We Could Be

VALERI BEATRIX

Dash&Keys Publishing

Chapter 1

The bartender looked like MC Hammer. Not the present day, bald and businesslike Hammer, but the top-of-his-game, "Too Legit to Quit" Hammer that rocked the curly box hair with the cuts in the sides. I fully expected him to conclude my drink order with an impromptu rendition of "Can't Touch This", but apparently table-dancing barkeeps were frowned upon. He slid me a shot of Tequila. My third.

"Do you rap?" I yelled above the music.

He smiled and shook his head no.

"Are you sure? Because you look just like MC Hammer."

"Who?"

My jaw dropped. Were there really people in the world who didn't know MC Hammer? That had to be a sin or a crime or something not good.

"I said—"

"Girl leave James alone before I tell him to cut you off."

I turned at the sound of Amara's voice in my ear.

"What! I was just asking a question. Can you believe he doesn't know who Hammer is?"

"Yes, now let's go. Our table's ready."

I gave her my best tipsy glare then stuck out my tongue. It was just like her to show up late then rush me. I tossed back the shot and tried not to wince when the sharp fluid scorched my throat. After leaving the bartender a generous tip, I bobbed along to the infectious House music as Amara squeezed us through the crowd and up to the VIP lounge. If I were smarter, I would have stayed in the office and sketched more of the mini-collection. Instead, I'd let the promise of free drinks lure me away. Now I was already half-drunk, and our evening had only just begun. Not a good sign.

I smiled anyway and held onto Amara's arm while she led us through the crowd of writhing bodies. She was barely over 5'0, but her commanding presence made people ignore her round, child-like features and move out of the way.

In no time, we reached the private bank of elevators that would take us to the clubs "sky boxes"—one of many perks associated with knowing the owner's daughter. Amara entered the code and we ascended to the sound of a lady singing about swinging from a chandelier.

We emerged from the elevator and into the dimly lit hall. Lights pulsed against its purple walls in erratic, seizure-inducing patterns, making me feel tipsier than I was. Best to focus my attention on the path ahead.

I saw his lips first. A luscious pair I'd only ever seen on movie screens or in fantasies. They parted as if to speak though I couldn't make out what amid the spectrum of lights flashing around us. My gaze flickered to the woman clinging to his arm. The over-sized breast on said woman. The body-con dress three years past its expiration date.

One step. Two steps. Three steps closer. I drank in his broad chest then looked up to find deep-set eyes taking me in: bare legs, Lanvin dress better suited for a runway than a club, bangs dusting my forehead. If he didn't like it, I couldn't tell as the intensity of his stare ignited a slow burn in my chest that worked its way through my body.

Before I knew what I was doing, my tongue lashed out to wet my lips, prompting his mouth into a mischievous smirk. I should have looked away. I would've looked away if only he released me. Instead, he stepped closer and closer still, until I could just touch the tips of his fingers with my own.

"No touching, miss."

"Huh?"

I looked down to see a burly hand gripping my outstretched arm. I might have protested had the owner of said arm *not* looked like a reject from the World Wrestling Federation.

"No touching Mr. Parker," WWF-man repeated.

"I wasn't, I just—"

"Girl, what is—" Amara turned around. "Sir, you need to unhand my friend."

"I will if she can keep her hands to herself."

"Keep what? Do you know who I—"

"No, he does not and let's keep it that way."

I gave a quick nod and pushed her forward, too embarrassed to peek at *Mr. Parker* again. Well, only when he was that close. I took a few more steps and turned back, but he'd disappeared. Was I hallucinating? A shiver crept through my skin and I concentrated on walking again, though my knees shuddered with every step.

Amara was already seated and opening the customary bottle of 2002 Dom Ruinart Champagne when I stepped in front of the glass table. It was much quieter upstairs where bottle service cost a month's rent, for some. Still, the bronze leather sectionals separated

6

by curtains of Swarovski crystals were full. Strangely enough, it was mostly women who populated the area.

I poured a glass of the bubbly stuff and raised it to a group sitting across from us.

"You know them?"

"Huh?"

"Do you know those women?" Amara asked.

"Oh, nah I was just…"

The sentence fell short. Any explanation I provided would probably get me a lecture anyway. I slid into the buttery soft leather couch and sipped the cool liquid. Familiar notes of apple and pear tickled my tongue as I thought of more important matters like my close encounter of the 1st kind with singer turned actor, turned model, making my head turn in search of him—Vince Parker.

It was normal to run into celebrities at Club Lynx, but rarely were they from the top tier of the A-list. I scooted deeper into the seat and pictured the smirk he'd offered.

"So, what happened with Brendan? All Nina said was you have an update." Amara's words slid through my brain in slow-motion.

I sat up straight and attempted to give her my full attention; tricky when the alcohol wanted me to do anything but.

"Oh, nothing really. We broke up."

"Ugh, I thought you had some real news," she crossed her arms.

"That—that is news!"

"Please, what's he, like, the 5th guy in six months?"

"Hey, give her a little credit. He actually made it past 30 days."

We looked up to see Nina McCullough—the third musketeer—smiling in a mint green dress that had to require oil to put on.

You're just jealous!

Was I? Probably. The curves on her body were impossible to achieve naturally, yet she'd done it. Her flawless skin was vampire pale despite a donation of melanin from her African-American mother. The first time we'd met in college, I couldn't stop staring. After we became friends, I learned it was a natural reaction from anyone who saw her, including young children and the elderly. She slid into the booth next to me and placed an arm around my bare shoulders.

"Let's try cheering her up for a change," she squeezed. "What do you say? Wanna get chocolate wasted?"

"Please don't start with the old movie quotes," Amara covered her ears.

7

"Why not? My friend is in a glass case of emotion right now."

"Here we go."

"I mean, just when I thought she couldn't get any dumber, she went and redeemed herself."

"Well, nobody's perfect," I played along.

"Except me. I wake up in the morning and piss excellence."

We turned to Amara and laughed. She always protested when we played "Quote 'em" but could never keep herself out of the game.

"See, you feel better now, right?" Nina asked.

"Wait, feel better?" Amara jumped in before I could respond. "Why does she—wait, did *he* dump *you*?"

In answer, I raised my empty glass then refilled it.

"Holy—wow, well, kudos to him."

"Hey!" I smacked her arm.

"What, you were gonna dump him anyway, weren't you?"

"Hmm," Nina said, ignoring the daggers I shot through my eyes. "I don't know about that. She did give him a key, and she actually bought him stuff."

"Wait, what? Why is this the first time I'm hearing about this?"

Nina and I offered knowing smirks.

"OK, nevermind that question, but seriously, you gave him a key to your place?"

"What I *gave* him was a key to the fabric studio and a few shirts to make him more presentable when we went out."

"Wow so does this mean you were actually into him?"

"No."

"Not even a smidge?" Nina asked.

It was my turn for the classic eye roll. I downed the dregs of my glass and placed it on the table. The warm fuzzies were taking over my body which meant I'd reached my limit. Plus, the action bought me time to figure out what to say. In truth, I'd felt more for Brendan than any of the others, but was I into him? Definitely not.

"I'm going to the bathroom," I said, concentrating on keeping my feet on the ground as I stood.

"Don't be like that, Sashimi," Nina put a hand on my back for support. "You know we just worry about you."

"Ok, first, and for the zillionth time, please stop calling me raw fish."

"Wait, Sashimi is raw fish?" Amara feigned ignorance.

"Technically, it's—"

"Nevermind," I said, easing back into the seat to get my

bearings.

Nina gave me the nickname the first day we met; said it was easier to remember my real name that way. But over 10 years had passed, and she still couldn't let it go.

"Like I said," Nina restarted, "we're just worried."

"Like I said, don't be, I mean, if I were a dude, we wouldn't even be having this conversation."

"True, but you're not a dude so here we are."

"No, here I go," I stood up.

"Damn, you're leaving like that?"

"I'm going to use the bathroom, unless you'd like to tell me how to do that as well."

"I mean, if you don't know by now—"

"Shut up, Amara," Nina grabbed her hand and pulled her up onto her feet. "We're coming with you"

The music was even louder when we re-entered the main level. I welcomed the bass that vibrated through my feet and up the rest of my body as we slowly navigated through the mass of party goers. Many a blouse had been ruined by red wine and other spirits, so we were extra careful to avoid the drunks.

We rounded the corner near the bar, and it was no surprise that every woman appeared to have synchronized their bladder with my own. Reluctantly, we took a place in the cramped line behind a woman yelling into her cell phone about seeing her best friend's boyfriend with someone else. *Men!*

"I don't know why you guys insist on using the common bathrooms. You know we can use the ones near my father's office."

"It's fine. We can wait." I told Amara, knowing it was a useless rebuttal.

"No, I don't think so!" She placed a hand on her hip. What she lacked in stature she more than made up for with attitude.

"Hey, maybe it'll go by fast."

"You're right. It will."

As she turned to fetch what we knew would be a bouncer, Nina and I tried to shield ourselves from the oncoming embarrassment.

"Lord, why do we even bother with this girl?"

"The free drinks, of course."

When Amara returned with two ultra-beefy security guards, we were still laughing.

"Ladies, there isn't that much piss in the world," she yelled down the corridor. Clusters of overly-wrought, scowling women turned around at the remark, but kept quiet when they noticed the

Incredible Hulk twins at her side.

"Do not make a scene tonight." Nina elbowed her in the ribs.

"Too late," I laughed.

With her henchmen in tow, Amara parted the sea of women and pulled us to the front of the line.

"I swear, somebody's going to beat your ass one day, and I hope I'm there to see."

"Please, these chicks wouldn't dare risk getting those lace-front wigs snatched out."

"OK, let's just pee and head back before something gets started," I suggested.

We used the restroom as quickly as possible. Afterwards, I checked my phone and was too caught up in an email to notice the new wall they'd put up.

"Dammit!"

I stubbed my toe and looked up to see it wasn't a wall, but Mr. WWF that I'd slammed into. I fought the urge to run.

"Excuse me miss, but could you come with me, please?"

"Now, why on Earth would I do that?" I asked, taking several steps back in case he tried something.

"My boss, Vince Parker, asked me to bring you and your friends to his table," he said, pointing over his shoulder. I peered at the faces behind him until I located that smile. Even from a distance it ignited the fire I'd felt earlier, though the handful of cheaply dressed women surrounding him quickly doused it.

It figures.

"Oh, now he wants to talk to her," Amara said, pulling me back.

I ignored her and turned toward Mr. Wrestle Mania. "Listen, I think I'll pass on your boss' request. It seems like he's already got his hands full."

From his raised eyebrow, he probably didn't hear that response often. I patted myself on the back.

"Oh, come on, Sashimi. I know you're upset, but you should go. It'll be fun," Nina chimed in.

"I have no interest in joining his groupie brigade. If you wanna meet him so badly, why don't you go up there?"

"Why don't we go up there and tell him that to his face?"

Amara tried pulling me around the guard, but he stepped up and blocked our path.

"Sorry, miss, but he asked for her specifically."

Uh oh. Wrong answer.

"Excuse me? Do you know who I am?" She jumped in front of him. "I own this club! I could toss you and your philandering boss out on your asses if I wanted to!"

It wasn't funny, but she looked too much like a Miniature Pinscher screaming at a Great Dane. Their cheer-me-up mission might possibly be accomplished.

"Oh, shut up, will you!" Nina spun her around while I mouthed "sorry" to the guy.

Hiding the disappointment, I scanned the crowd, trying to decipher the best way to head back. Sure, it always seemed easy. Squeeze through here or push past there, but I knew the minute we moved, everyone else would too. I'd finally decided on the least dangerous route, when I saw him.

Brendan.

Wearing a Gucci shirt I'd given him for his birthday— the only piece of his wardrobe that didn't come from Marshalls. By his side was a long-legged, wannabe model-type, though she'd likely never reach the aspiration.

"What's the hold up?" Nina leaned over my shoulder to see what was going on.

Three gasps sounded, though I was sure mine was for a different reason. My heart's reaction to seeing him was embarrassing; as if it didn't recall the tech-assisted, break-up message we'd received not two hours ago. On the other hand, my brain quickly ran through a list of legal ways to hurt him.

Nina grabbed my arm and jerked me in the opposite direction, "Keep walking."

"No! Walk right up to him so he can see how good you look," Amara encouraged.

"In other words, be petty and stoop to his level."

"It's not petty, it's…"

The rest of their conversation registered on some level in my brain, but I didn't have the focus to keep up with it. All I could feel was the moisture forming in my palms, the steady increase of breath and the screeching voice in my brain.

Bastard! That's why you broke up with me.

"I'll…be back."

I didn't wait for their approval. With a heart thudding louder than the base, I pushed through the crowd. I fully intended to march up to him and bloody his nose, but my feet turned at the last minute and headed back to the restroom. The line was still long so I settled for resting against the wall to ease the dizziness that

11

suddenly felt it would envelope me. Why in the world was I reacting this way to some jerk who could barely buy me a decent bottle of wine? A guy I'd proclaimed nothing more than a plaything 30 minutes ago. Must be the rejection, I decided. No one liked being benched and replaced so easily.

"Are you alright?" A deep, sensuous voice— like fingertips caressing my spine— slid through my thoughts. I lifted my head to see Vince Parker staring down at me with his bodyguard not far behind. His outfit was simple: black Henley shirt and dark blue jeans. Still, he couldn't have been sexier if he'd worn nothing.

Again, that feeling in my chest.

Again, the itch to reach out and touch him. I shook my head to free myself from his hold and stood up straight.

"I'm fine. Thank you."

There, I'd said it without sounding like the star-struck teen dancing in my brain. But what was this reaction? I'd met famous people before. Plenty of them.

They weren't as edible, though.

"Are you sure you're ok?" He stepped closer.

Close enough to smell. Close enough to touch. Close enough to make me wish he'd close the space between us. As if he'd lifted the thoughts from my mind, he reached for me. My pulse quickened as I waited for the sensation of his hand against mine.

"Can't touch this."

A small hand appeared and pulled me away. I glanced back as she eased us through the crowd. His hand hovered in mid-air. His eyes smoldered as if his prize had been stolen.

Brunch. Church. Shopping. Splayed out in my California King with a trashy novel. All acceptable ways to spend a weekend, but I'd done neither of those sensible activities. No, I'd given in to peer-pressure and allowed my friends— and an unsuspecting Uber driver— to shuttle me from bar to bar. Like all bad ideas it seemed good at the time, and as I stood in the foyer of my SoHo showroom shielding myself from the blinding LED lights, I knew I had to exercise better judgment.

Securing a travel carton of coffee cups, I waved to the receptionist and trudged up the concrete steps that led to my main office. At the top of the stairs, I'd normally pause to stare out on the maze-like structure of the offices below, but I instead pushed through the frosted glass doors and found my assistant—London Park, smiling cheerfully.

"Anyeonghase— ooh, for me?" London reached towards the carton.

"Not so loud, and please, it is too early for Korean 101."

"How else are you going to learn?"

"I'm not."

I shrugged out of my jacket then traded it for a turquoise Pashmina from my closet. London snickered and sipped from one of the cups.

"Mleh, what is this, tar?"

"Coffee. Drink it. Appreciate it," I brushed past her. "Did the samples arrive?"

"Umm, yes. Two dresses, three shirts and all the pants. We're still waiting for the printed Viscose though," she said, resting the carton on my desk. "So, let me guess, Brendan broke up with you, right?"

"What are you talking about?"

"You only drink coffee if you're hung-over and you only get drunk when someone breaks up with you."

I stared at her as she flipped through a pile of sketches on my desk. Either she was way too perceptive, or I'd established an unhealthy relationship pattern. Pride had me going with option one.

"*Anyway*, we don't have time for this." I glanced at my watch. "We've got models to cast, or did you forget about the fashion show?"

"Of course not, it's just that—"

"If the next words out of your mouth aren't related to this job in some way, you're fired."

London closed her mouth then pretended to zip it shut.

"Good, now pull the toiles for any collection samples that haven't arrived and meet me downstairs." I grabbed the IPAD and a folder of swatches from my desk then headed out. I could feel London making faces behind me, but I'd have to deal with her later. At present my main concern was finalizing plans for the mini fashion show and store opening.

After years of building private clientele that included a number of A-listers through social media, I'd risked my reputation and copious amounts of money from both lenders and investors by launching my first collection. The success of the line was more than I'd imagined. With a retail store in the works and the bar set, the pressure was on to maintain it.

"Hey, you forgot your breakfast," London called down.

"Fine, fine. Bring it with you."

Downstairs, my heels clicked across the polished concrete floor as I hurried to the back entrance of my workroom. As expected, models waited in clusters amid a backdrop of dress forms, fabric bolts and clothing racks. With Fashion Week recently concluded, the pool of models was much larger as many had come in from all over the world. At my drafting table, I pushed a pile of sketches to the side, took a few bites of a cream cheese bagel and called for the first model.

Tall and thin with Eastern European features, she placed her portfolio and composite card detailing her measurements on the table. I flipped through the book then had the young lady demonstrate her walk or what turned out to be a high-stepping horse stomp. I thanked her, placed her card in what would be the "no" pile, and called for the next person. It was going to be a long day.

Castings were supposed to be the easiest part of creating a runway show, but for me they were the most stressful. So many factors determined whether a model was right for the collection, many of them intangible. Like the first model, she might have a great face, but the wrong walk. Or a great walk, but a body that didn't hold the clothes well. Then again, she could have the body, the walk, and the face, but command an astronomical fee.

As the morning faded into afternoon, my earlier prediction proved true. I'd seen a number of girls but had only cast half of what I needed. I sifted through the "maybe" pile then sat back. Beside me, Nina scrubbed a hand over her face. She'd been in the room for all of five minutes, but already she'd crossed both arms and legs, signaling she was over it.

"Seriously, of all the girls we've seen, you only like--" she shuffled through a small stack of cards displaying photos of the women as well as their measurements, "Eight! You've been here for over four hours and you've only picked eight?"

"Correction: 10." I directed her attention to two photos taped to one of several white boards behind us.

"Big whoop."

"I even have a "maybe" pile."

"Please, we all know what happens to the maybes."

"Well, I told you not to sit in for the casting, didn't I?"

She was right, though I'd never admit it. The girls I'd found so far were ok, but what we needed was a *name*. If I wanted to attract more A-list clientele, I needed someone they'd recognize. I pinched the bridge of my nose and called for the next girl.

"Are we almost done?"

"Nina darling, no one is holding you against your will. I'm sure there's something you can do besides riding my nerves."

"Nah, I need to stay here and make sure you stay on task," she said.

"You mean on budget."

"That too," she poked my arm. "So, have you gotten over Vince yet?"

"Wait— what are you talking about?"

"You were blabbing about him all weekend. His luscious mouth. His bedroom eyes. That body. The more you drank, the more you kept talking about him."

"I don't know what you're talking about."

And I really didn't. I thought back over the weekend's events but being pulled away from him was the last thing I remembered clearly. An act of treason I'd yet to punish Amara for.

"You don't know? I'll show you."

"What? You didn't…"

I motioned for the next girl to wait as Nina pulled up a recording on her phone. We were at a bar—which one, I couldn't say. I sat at a counter; the customary rows of liquor lined the wall behind me. Nearby patrons either gawked at or ignored me completely as a rambled on about meeting the finest, most famous man on Earth and blowing it without really *blowing it*. Video me then launched into ways in which I *could* blow it, but I quickly turned it off.

"Dude, how could you let me get that drunk?"

"I keep telling you, when you're—"

"No, nevermind," I shook my head. "We'll discuss this later."

The model continued, and the process started all over again: Portfolio, comp-card, walk. Yes, no, maybe. Now though, I couldn't focus like before. My mind kept going back to the video then further back to the scene of the crime. Hindsight wanted me to believe I should have accepted Vince's offer to join him, but I knew better. Why be one of a number who'd already said yes instead of the only to say no. Yes, I'd made the right decision. Right?

By the time we finished, I couldn't tell one face from another. Luckily, I didn't have to. With the "maybe" pile in hand, I stood up and reached for the sky, groaning as the tension released its hold on my muscles. A yoga session was definitely in order.

15

"Hold up." Nina grabbed me before I could walk away. "Go through these maybes and make a few yeses, would you? Preferably the new girls—they're cheaper."

"Is that all you care about? The bottom line?"

"Umm, yes! If I left it to you, we'd still be in your condo sewing clothes and making cold calls instead of in this wonderful place."

Sarcasm laced her voice as she glanced around my office—affectionately named the Mullet for its sophisticated front upstairs, and the concrete-floored, exposed brick back (for workspace and the occasional party). Except now it was more like after the party, when all the guests were gone, and you're left with a slew of red cups, beer bottles and left-over food to clean. In this case, the mess took the form of fabric bolts, clothing racks, mood boards, and sketches. Sketches on tables. Pinned onto cork boards. Taped up on the walls. Organized chaos.

"For the record, my father is the reason we have this place," I said as we walked through the hall and up the stairs to the more presentable office. "By the way, how was the meeting with Paul Rosen?"

The guy was a gazillionaire who normally backed tech start-ups, but I'd met his daughter through Instagram and she helped set up the meeting.

"When he was able to focus on the numbers instead of staring at me, he seemed impressed."

"I keep telling you. It's a sad reality, but we'd probably do better hiring a man to talk to these guys. You're just too sexy," I slapped her on the back. "Even with a buzz cut."

"Shut up!"

I grabbed two empty cork boards from their resting place against the wall and started tacking on the comp-cards of both the yes and maybe group. The maybe board was nearly full when London burst through doors.

"Umm ladies, we have one more model," she said, smiling wide enough for me to see her molars.

"Did you tell her casting finished 30 minutes ago?"

"I thought of that, but I think you might want to come down."

Nina and I shared a look then followed her back into the main area. A lean, statuesque woman stood browsing through a rack of samples. She paused at each one, carefully running her fingers over the fabric.

"Umm, hello?"

16

"Oh," she jumped at the sound of my voice. "I didn't you hear you guys. Too caught up admiring the merchandise."

A gasp tumbled from my lips as I clutched invisible pearls. I'd seem them before: the wide, doe eyes, the long nose, the sharp cheekbones directing like arrows to a full mouth. I'd seen them all before but never up close. I'd met a few celebrities before and had never been star-struck (until recently) but standing in front of Daniela Harrington—the one model I'd dreamed of working with forever—took all the words. Nina and London seemed equally mystified.

"I'm so sorry I'm late, you must be Sasha," she said, extending a hand.

"Umm, yes, hi," I stammered, moving closer to return the gesture.

"It's great to meet you. Again, I'm sorry I'm late. I had every intention of being here on time, but things are so different from when I used to live here. Guess life really does go on, huh? Oh right," she dug into the messenger bag draped on her shoulder.

"For you," she said, holding out a portfolio.

"Wait, I'm sorry are you—are you here for *casting*?"

"Of course, that is unless you've booked everyone already."

"Oh no, no, it's just I didn't expect to see *the* Daniela Harrington, *here*."

She shook her head and smiled the famous smile that left lipstick and toothpaste aisles bare. Rumors swirled about why she'd fled the modeling scene four years ago, but I didn't care. She was back, and she was here.

"So umm, should I walk or..." she glanced around.

"Oh, right, right, this way."

I took her portfolio and handed it to Nina. Though I didn't need to see her book or her walk to know I'd cast her, I slowly flipped through the pages anyway, so I wouldn't appear as eager as I felt. After her walk, I chose a teal, a-lined wrap dress for her to try.

"London, pen the hem up an inch. Let's see how it looks."

"Ne, sangjungnim."

I shook my head. The girl insisted on speaking Korean no matter how much I insisted my brain couldn't support a fourth language. London slung the camera over her shoulder and hurried over. Slender in black cigarette pants and an over-sized gray sweater, she could have easily been auditioning, too. Well, maybe if her five-foot frame didn't need an assist from the sky-high boots she wore as naturally as her own feet. With the new hem-length in place, she shooed Daniela to the photo wall and snapped a picture.

London rushed to my side and showed me the image on the camera's screen. "Is she really auditioning for our show?" she asked.

"Can we afford her?"

I pursed my lips as the air seeped out of my invisible bubble. Our budget was already tighter than a waist-trainer. We had a presentation for new investors lined up but didn't guarantee we'd have enough to do pay her. Daniela finished her photos, rushed over and squeezed my arm.

"This collection is beautiful, sort of a 90s, East meets West vibe."

"Uh, someone who gets it," I said, jabbing Nina in the arm before turning my attention back to the matter at hand.

"So, I'm truly grateful you came by today and I'd love nothing more than to cast you, but honestly I'm not sure we have that kind of money right now."

Daniela laughed and touched my arm. "You've heard the rumors, I suppose. The astronomical fees, the diva behavior, etc. All lies." Darkness slid into her features though the smile remained.

"The truth is, I need this just as much as you do. Your brand is in a decent position now, but I know you need this show to be a success in order to solidify your presence. As for me, I wasn't gone a month before they'd crowned a new "it" model. If I want to get back to the top, I have to do something they'd never expect."

"Like working with a lesser known brand," Nina offered.

"Exactly!"

"Well, does that mean we'll get a discounted rate?"

"Nina!" I slapped her arm.

"What? You know how some of them get! Giving a sob story to soften you up then hit you with the five-figure fee!"

"Ok, but you didn't have to—"

"It's ok," Daniela said, "I totally understand and am willing to negotiate something we all can agree to."

"No time like the present," Nina said.

I pinched the bridge of my nose, but Daniela just laughed and followed Nina to her office. When they were out of sight, London seized my arm like a toddler in a toy store.

"Can we keep her, please?"

"That's up to our budget, shoe-string as it is."

More like half a shoe string, really. Still, if anyone could work a financial miracle it was Nina.

For that reason, I refocused my attention and flipped through the remaining polaroids. I even added a few more to the "yes" pile. London and I tacked them to a white board to see how the women looked as a group. Nina and Daniela returned from their "meeting", giggling like they were old friends, just as we posted the last photo. Daniela gave a quick wave, collected her personal items and left while Nina slid into the chair beside me.

"Are we done here?" she asked, reaching up to pull fingers through nonexistent hair. She'd shaved it ten years ago after her first divorce, but still forgot from time to time. That is unless someone made the mistake of comparing her to a certain video vixen. Then they'd get a mouthful on how said vixen was merely a cheap knock-off.

"We're done, but seriously. Did that just happen? Did Daniela Harrington just audition for *my* show? I mean, did we book her? Can we pay her? Oh, and what had ya'll *guffawing* like best friends?"

"What is this, the Black Archie comic? Who even says *guffaw*?"

"Oh, shut up and answer the question!"

"Which one? There were like—"

"Ok, this is too cray-cray," London suddenly appeared in front of us.

"Are we still saying cray?"

"Shush, you," she jabbed a finger at Nina. "We have a new client!"

Nina and I shared a glance.

"O-K, but you know we're not accepting anyone new until after the store opening?"

"I know, but it's through Misha May. She said it's an emergency. She needs to borrow whatever we can spare for a photo shoot. Nothing has to be custom."

If it had been anyone else I would've turned them down, but Misha May was the first stylist to introduce my pieces to her clients. One social media post from her did more for my brand in ten minutes than I'd been able to do in year.

"Fine. When does she need them?"

"Umm, now?"

"Now!" Nina and I responded.

"Who does she need this for?"

"Well, she wouldn't say. Only that the client has an emergency and could really use our help. They're willing to pay," London rubbed her hands together and smiled.

"Pay? Who pays to use samples?"

19

"Who looks a gift horse in the mouth?" was Nina's in character response. We needed the money, but it all seemed a bit sketchy. In general, no one paid to use something if they could get it for free. Then again, perhaps they realized the inconvenience of their request and wanted to make amends. Whatever the case, I wasn't in a position to turn down free money.

"Alright, London. Grab a few pieces and take them over but stay and make sure there's no funny business going on. Oh, and take Kara with you."

"She's already gone for the day. So is everyone else who could be useful...except you two."

"Don't look at me. All I know is numbers," Nina said, backing towards the door.

"Fine."

I glanced at the wall clock and hoped whoever this client was would be worth losing a quiet night at home.

Chapter 2

When we reached our destination over an hour later— a warehouse in Hempstead, I didn't have to ask London if she'd known the shoots location. The fact that she'd pretended to sleep as soon as we entered the vehicle said enough. I also didn't have to tell her she'd taken another step towards the unemployment line. My posture did the talking as I folded my arms and watched her unload several garment bags of clothes by herself.

"Some assistance would be nice," she said.

"It would, wouldn't it?"

I squeezed her shoulder then headed into the large, ash gray building. I wrinkled my nose as the smell of sawdust and liquor welcomed me when I stepped inside. Despite the odor, the interior— with its gleaming wood floors and exposed red brick— looked newly renovated. The muffled sound of music emanated from the floor above us and I headed for the elevator.

"Seriously, you're not going to help me?" London asked, her head barely visible above the garment bags. I watched her teeter from side to side and gave in. She was the best assistant I'd ever had, and I didn't want to lose her over a few bags of clothes.

"Come on," I said, grabbing one from the stack.

Since Misha hadn't told us exactly where to go once we arrived, we took the elevator to the top floor. The doors opened, and we stepped into a pristine white hallway, with concrete floors not unlike those in my office. Teardrop light bulbs hung from wood beams lining the ceiling and gave the area a warm glow. Combined with the rumbling 808 of whatever song was playing, it felt like we were entering a club.

I'd never been to a video shoot, but I'd imagined them to be more hectic than the scene we came upon. The room was the size of a basketball court, though only half of it was in use. Floor to ceiling windows covered the walls and bathed the room in the fading rays of twilight. Straight ahead, a contraption that resembled a mini train-track lined the floor and a mounted camera rolled along the rails. At least four men with cameras jockeyed for positions as they circled someone. I peered around them to get a better glimpse, but no luck there.

"Sasha!"

A voice called just as the music stopped. I turned to see Misha hurrying towards us. Even with the chilly September weather, she wore a six-pack bearing cropped top, cut-off shorts and a silk Kimono-like robe. Her hair, now shaved on one side, was ruby red instead of the bleached blond I remembered.

"Oh my gosh, thank you so much for coming," she said, pulling me in for a hug. "D&G flaked out on me, the bastards. Apparently, an editorial in Vogue is more important than an R&B video shoot."

"How dare they?" I feigned surprise. "You should have called me in the first place."

"And what, hear your usual line about having only one set of collection samples?"

London giggled beside me. I tried to elbow her ribs, but the bags were in the way.

"Anyway, I'm here now, despite my unfinished sketches, incomplete samples, unfinished store…I could go on."

"Please don't," Misha said, laughing. "I totally appreciate you being here, and I can't wait 'til I'm able to just buy your stuff instead of begging for freebies."

"Wait, you get freebies?" London asked, adjusting the samples in her arms.

While they continued to chat about what they did and did not get from me, I tried again to locate the star of the occasion. From the song they'd played I knew it was a man. The voice was vaguely familiar but didn't set off any memory bells in my head.

"Sasha, come. Let me show you around."

I instructed London to add the samples to a nearby clothing rack, and guard them with her life. Misha led me through a group of scantily clad women to a section cordoned off by several Shoji screens. Behind them was a table full of accessories and shoes, more racks of clothing and around 30 women. *It figures.*

A few of them huddled together, vying for a space in the mirror of a brightly lit vanity. Others readjusted skirts or dresses, clearly made to fit their younger siblings.

"They're waiting for the club scene," Misha whispered.

I nodded my agreement, though I'd never seen women dressed like that in any of the clubs I'd been to. Then again, I didn't exactly get out much.

"It seems like you have everything covered. Why do you need more?" I wondered aloud.

"It's for the principal model of this shoot. They want her to have an edgy, but polished—"

"Playback!"

A male voice yelled, startling and prompting me to turn around. The song started again, and the camera moved along the makeshift tracks until it came to rest in front of a shirtless male with skin like fresh ginger snaps. The definition in his abs was clear a distance and I felt like one of Pavlov's dogs, salivating at the mouth.

"Delicious, isn't he?" Misha said, reading my mind.

"Who is it?"

"Come on," Misha pulled my arm. "I'll show you."

We followed the tracks. The mystery man had moved to stand before one of the windows. Outside, the sun retreated and bathed both his silhouette and the room in a hazy orange glow. The cameras panned around as a woman appeared and sauntered towards him. I frowned when she placed a possessive hand on his shoulder. He turned and as the orange rays highlighted his profile— strong jaw, sleek nose, full lips— I stifled a gasp.

"Can you believe it? *The* Vince Parker?" Misha nudged my side. "Isn't he gorgeous in person?"

Yes. Yes, he is.

The model's hands caressed the muscles of his chest then slowly worked their way to the indention on his hips. He smiled and placed a palm against her face then brought their foreheads together. Her chest swelled. Lips parted. Eyes closed. He leaned towards her. Inched towards her mouth until he was close enough to touch it with his tongue.

"Cut!"

The director yelled, and Vince immediately disengaged. I, on the other hand, could not return to reality so quickly. The heat in my body could not be tempered so quickly. Every time he touched her, every caress of her body with his gaze felt like an act against me. When his lips advanced toward hers, it was I who anticipated their touch.

Get real! He's out of your league and a player to boot!

"Hello, earth to Sasha."

"Oh, sorry." I brought my attention back to the real world.

"Did you get caught up in the fine-ness? It's ok, it happens all the time."

"No, no, it's not that, it just seemed so *real*."

"He didn't win a Golden Globe for nothing," Misha said, laughing. "Come on, I'll introduce you."

"Umm, no that's ok. I think—"

"Just come on. I have to adjust his pants, anyway," she said, wiggling her brows.

She dragged me by the arm through a group of cameramen.

"Won't you get in trouble for interrupting?" I asked, trying to stall the inevitable though I had no clue why.

"What am I, five? Besides, I'm doing him a favor."

Vince sat in a director's chair reviewing the footage they'd recorded through a screen on the back of the camera. Two women hovered behind him. One massaged his shoulders while the other removed his shoes and replaced them with another pair. *The groupie brigade!*

His voice was the perfect blend of bass and honey as he insisted they reshoot the last scene. *Something's not right*, he'd said though he probably just wanted to cop another feel.

Misha peeked over his shoulder while I stood in the back. "No, definitely not perfect," she said.

"What's missing?"

"Well, no offense, but it looks a bit too 'let me hit it' as opposed to the 'we're in love' vibe you're going for."

"You're right. It needs something else...someone—," Vince stood up and pulled one of the girls to stand in front of him then motioned for her to turn around. He grinned as she moved in a slow circle but shook his head.

"No, not you," he said.

The other woman was asked to do the same and she too was deemed "unworthy". He sent them both on their way and was about to take a seat when he glanced in my direction.

"Who are you?" he asked, offering the full force of his attention.

If the unnatural curves of the women on set were an indication of his taste, then I would be cast off the island. I had a great set of breasts— so I'd been told— but they didn't qualify for the "big" label.

He stalked towards me; 6'0'' of well-muscled determination. With his shirt off, he was taller than I remembered. Just like the first time, I couldn't keep myself from wandering over his body. I couldn't keep my mind from rolling towards the gutter.

His attention finally landed on me and while a number of

emotions flickered over his face, recognition wasn't one of them.

Told ya! Did you really think he'd remember you? Maybe it's the makeup, I reasoned. My club look was much more glam than my everyday work look. *Sure, that's it…the makeup.*

"Are you a dancer?" he asked.

"Why would you—where did that come from?"

"Your feet," he pointed down. "Most ballet dancers I know stand with their feet in that position."

I looked down at my out-turned feet and tried to remember the last time I'd danced. At one point in my life, I'd have to be dragged from the studio kicking and screaming. Now, I couldn't recall the last time I'd even considered putting on Pointe shoes; hell, I didn't even know where they were.

"Well, yeah, I umm—"

"Vince, she's not here for that. She's the designer I got the samples from, Sasha Ellis," Misha interrupted.

"Sasha," he said.

I'd heard it many times before, but never in such honeyed tones that left me ready to drop it all: guards, pretense…clothes.

That's probably how all these women ended up here.

"Can you help me with something?" he asked.

"Help you with what?"

Boobs. They were the first thing I noticed when I turned at the sound of the voice behind me. At least an F cup and covered in— what was that, latex? Seriously? The woman from the scene offered a smile and weighed herself against me. I wasn't as curvy, but what I did have was neatly packaged in a leather pencil skirt, fitted sweater and camel coat: business sexy. The smile brightened, but the tension remained in her jaw. No, we definitely weren't going to be friends.

"Oh, what's up, Martinique," Vince said. "This is Sasha."

With exaggerated slowness, she moved to his side and placed a hand on his bicep. I thought her breasts were big, but there were no words for her behind. Ten years ago, I might have been impressed by its ample size, but these days anyone with a credit card could charge an ass to it. There was even the riskier, low-budget option of butt shots. Hers looked a bit uneven so I counted her among the latter group.

"Nice to meet you," she said, flipping the long side of her bobbed hair across a shoulder.

"Likewise," I lied.

"We're going to try a scene with Sasha," Vince informed her

25

She made a sound as if she were about to throw up. "I'm sorry, what? You can't just pull some chick off the street and throw her in a video."

That's probably what he did with you! I wanted to say but opted for the less-traveled high road. I had better things to do with my time. Speaking of, I glanced at my watch then located London— standing guard near the rack with her cell phone trained in our direction. *This girl!*

"Alright, well…I'll be going." I moved towards her, but a hand caught my elbow and sent shock-waves through my veins.

"Come on. You know you wanna help me out," Vince said.

I tried to step forward, but my feet weren't listening. Shifting to look at him, I found the full force of his Hollywood smile beaming down at me, and dark eyes daring me to say no.

Chapter 3

"I still can't believe you said no to Vince Parker," Amara said, attempting a standing knee pose for the third time before tumbling onto her mat.

"Believe it," I said, though I couldn't believe it either.

At the time, it felt good to turn down the offer to be in his video, especially with that cocky grin of his. But now...maybe it was a good night's rest or the clarity that came with sweating out toxins and useless thoughts, but it felt like I'd made a huge mistake. Then again, hindsight wasn't always 20/20. Maybe I'd made the right decision after all.

Beside me, Amara sprawled out onto her mat and chugged on a bottle of water. I'd tried to warn her that yoga in a room set at 105 degrees was a bad idea for beginners, but her need to know what had transpired between Vince and I overruled her good sense. We'd barely gone through two postures and already she'd settled into a pile of sweat on the floor.

After another 60 minutes of deep breathing and postures (Amara remained on her mat and created playlists for Spotify) we hit the showers and headed out into the chilly morning. Since the yoga studio wasn't far from my office, I opted to give my muscles an extra stretch by walking.

"Can I just say, you have the worst judgment when it comes to guys. Which is strange, considering the fact that you never really commit to any of them. On top of that though, you flip out over him if he's broke, but let him have a little bit of money and you avoid him like he's a leper. What's more, you have the nerve to complain when—"

A long set of jet-black dreadlocks jump-started my pulse as we maneuvered the sidewalk. Feelings I thought had come and gone regenerated themselves like mutating cells. I tried looking around the other pedestrians for a better view but had no luck. Speeding up would only make her suspicious, but what else could I do?

"Sasha! Did you hear me?"

"Huh, oh yeah, you're right."

"Good. I'll see you later then."

I gave her a quick hug then turned to continue my search, but the man was gone.

The disappearing man was still on my mind when I reached the office, but there was no time left to ruminate over who he *might* have been with the investors meeting due to start.

"Happy Thursday!" London called when I pushed through the double doors of the conference room.

"Are the packets ready for the presentation?"

"Good morning to you too and yes, everything is here," she gestured to the folders, sitting like placemats in front of each chair along with a notepad and bottle of water.

"Looks good. Did you remember to put—"

"Yes! The Spring samples are in the showroom along with print outs of the mini collection. I also laid out our best sellers from the current collection and those from last season."

I smiled. A good assistant was hard to find, especially one that you didn't have to explain everything to. In the four years since I'd started the company, I'd gone through 13 assistants before finding her.

"Great! You've done everything except…"

"Crap! Your tea! I left it in the kitchenette! BRB!"

"Stop using acronyms!"

I took a moment to go through my notes. Second to castings, "money meetings" were the most stressful parts of business. Convincing people to part with their well-earned cash was the equivalent of asking for their first born.

The intercom buzzed: "Ms. Ellis, the clients are here."

"Great. Give me five minutes then send them in."

With a deep breath, and a silent prayer, I readied my smile for the people that would shape the rest of my career.

"As you can see, our numbers are up 22% from last year's quarter and 9% from last month. If sales remain steady, we're on pace to double our earnings from last year."

As Nina—our VP of Sales—explained the company's profit margins, I tried to gauge the client's thoughts. Capital Investment Group was known to be selective in what they chose to put their money into. Truthfully, I was surprised they were even interested as they too normally funded tech start-ups, but I shouldn't have been surprised. Nina could sell water to a well.

Still, the best read I could make from their expressions was somewhere between sleepy and remotely interested... or was that boredom? I was still trying to figure it out when the intercom buzzed. I frowned and motioned for London to answer.

"Evelyn, Ms. Ellis asked not to be interrupted."

"It better be an emergency," I mumbled through clenched teeth.

"There's an investor who says he's supposed to be in this meeting."

"Huh?" I looked around the room. As far as I knew, everyone was accounted for. Maybe it was an additional member to their team.

"Fine, send them in."

London relayed the message and placed the phone down quietly.

"Sorry for the interruption everyone. It seems we have one—" I stopped short when the door opened. Wearing a blue, Tom Ford suit and a brilliant smile, Vince Parker strolled into the room as if it was his name on the doors.

"I apologize for my lateness. You wouldn't believe the traffic out there," he joked.

Everyone perked up in their seats and laughed. Vince winked as he took the empty chair across from me then clasped his hands together and faced Nina. She looked to me for answers, but I was just as confused. When the group settled down, she returned to the presentation.

I tried to pay attention as well, but kept turning back to him. *What is he doing here?* A better question was how did he know to come here? I wanted to be upset that he'd intruded in my professional matters, but anger couldn't contend with the butterflies fluttering in my stomach.

"I'll give the floor back to Ms. Ellis."

I started at the sound of my name then quickly stood up.

"Thanks Nina. If everyone will follow me to the showroom, our Production team has some beautiful samples from the upcoming collections."

I wrung my hands while leading them to the showroom. Knowing Vince Parker would view my presentation only heightened the nervousness. When we finally entered the area—an ode to modernism composed of steel, polished white marble and glass—I'd managed to tune him out and settle back into myself. Now and then I'd turn and catch him drinking in parts of my body—sending invisible tremors that paused my speech.

"So," I concluded. "Questions? Comments?"

After answering a round of queries, I turned the meeting over to the production team and inched towards the back. While there, I tried to get Vince's attention, but he seemed to have a genuine interest in their presentation.

The meeting wrapped up and though there were a few more questions for me, the investors were most interested in chatting with Vince. I watched as he charmed them with his smile and easy humor. When they said their goodbyes, I was certain of two things:

1. I'd receive more money that we'd asked for.

2. Vince Parker was sexy as hell.

He stood with hands in his pockets, blending into the backdrop of my showroom like an ad campaign. A moment of silence passed between us before he cleared his throat and stepped forward.

"Sorry again for the interruption. It wasn't part of the plan."

"There was a plan?"

"I'll get to that, but first why didn't you tell me we'd met the other night at Minx?"

He remembers! My heart leapt at the thought before I instructed it to keep its feet on the ground.

"I didn't think you'd recall."

"Honestly, I didn't until you turned me down at the shoot. It was strange for that to happen twice in a week," he said, stepping closer. "So, I thought back to that night. I have to say you look different in your work clothes."

He gestured to my ensemble: black, wide legged trousers paired with a fitted, white lace top. Though flattered by his attention, it was clear why he'd turned up. I presented a challenge and if there was one thing men loved, it was a great chase sequence. Still, I couldn't help considering what it would be like to play along.

"Well, now that your curiosity is satisfied, I'll walk you out," I said, not waiting for him to follow.

"Wait a minute. I want to invest in Sashelle Ltd."

"And just what do you know about Sashelle Ltd.?"

He cleared his throat. "Well, I know that you and your good friend, Nina, started it shortly after you earned your M.A. from Central St. Martins."

"How did you—"

"Let me finish!" he cut in. "I also know you started by sending one-of-kind pieces to NYC's "it girls", and from there moved to small boutiques and eventually to stores like Saks and Nordstrom.

Now you're in the process of opening your first flagship store in SoHo! How's that?"

"Wow. Your Google skills are impressive." I felt the smirk before I could stop it. Gone were the days when a man had to do more than point and click to learn my life story.

"Well hey, if I'm going to invest in something, I need to know if there's potential for a speedy return."

I paused at this statement then continued up the stairs to my office. When we passed the front desk, I sneered at Evelyn and mouthed the words: *I'm gonna kill you!*

"Oh wait, Ms. Ellis there's—"

"Not now, Evelyn," I called over my shoulder.

"You know, I should—" the sentence fell short as Vince and I entered my office to find our Senior Patter Maker, Nan Yen pacing in front of my desk. With a deep breath, I steeled my nerves and inserted a smile.

"Nan, what brings you here?"

Though I could already guess. She was the eternally smiling, gentle-natured type—until you messed with her work.

"Ms. Sasha, you know I don't make trouble but, please, can you make up your mind about the 'Vixen' dress?" she said in Mandarin. "I cannot make samples if you keep changing."

"I know, I know, I'm sorry. I promise this will be the last change, I think."

"Ms. Sasha!"

"Ok, ok, tell you what," I escorted her to the door. "How about I get you some tickets to a show or game or something."

"Ok, you do that, I make exception this time."

"Good, London," I handed her off, grateful she hadn't thrown anything this time, "get the lady what she wants!"

"Wow."

I jerked around. I'd forgotten Vince was there. He stood with arms folded across his chest, with lips pulled into that sexy smirk.

"What?"

"Nothing, you just…" he walked closer. "I didn't know you speak Mandarin."

"Oh no? Didn't that show up in your search?"

"No, and I'm kind of glad because seeing that just turned me on…wait, did I just say that out loud?" he stepped back and swiped a hand over his face. "My bad, Sasha. That was rude of me."

A flash of heat crossed my cheeks, but I played it cool. I should've made it clear what he could do with the fresh remarks, but because seeing him in that suit aroused the same feeling in me I kept my mouth shut.

"It's fine, but tell me, what are you really doing here?" I moved to stand in front of him.

"I told you I want to invest, but I also wanted to invite you to a performance this weekend."

I sat at my desk to put some distance between us. It was easier to gauge his sincerity if I couldn't feel the air vibrating between us.

"You could have just called the office."

"True, but I wouldn't have been able to see you again."

I twirled a strand of hair at the nape of my neck and tried not to blush. It was too bad my body never complied with my brain in these matters.

"Look, I know you thought I was trying to add you to my "groupie brigade", but really I just wanted a chance to talk to you."

"So, you admit there is a groupie brigade?"

Before he could respond, London appeared just behind him.

"Sorry to interrupt, but Jana from Gilt is on the line."

"OK, give me a minute."

I turned to Vince, struggling to suppress the grin that tickled the corners of my mouth.

"Well," I began, walking him out. "I'm happy you stopped by today, but the next time you'd like to see me, please make an appointment first."

Vince laughed, "Wow, really?"

"No, not really," I smiled. "I'm just saying that while I'm sure your presence was more than welcome in there today, I take my business very seriously and would—"

"Say no more," he interrupted. "You're right. I should have waited until you were finished," he grabbed my hand and pulled me closer, instantly raising my pulse. He really had a problem with boundaries.

"It's just—I really wanted to see you."

"Well, I guess I can't argue with that logic." No matter how cheesy it seemed.

"No, you certainly can't." He kissed my hand.

London cleared her throat, causing us both to start.

"Sorry, but you know Jana gets a little restless."

"Right. O.K." I turned to Vince. "I'm sorry, but I have to take this call."

"No problem. So, I'll see you Friday, right?"

"Maybe," I said, trying not to smile at the prospect.

"Ok well," he took a blue post-it and scribbled something down. "Here's my number. Give me a call if you decide to show up."

Chapter 4

If I'd known Vince's concert involved Lil' Money and friends, I would have taken a rain check. Who was I kidding? I would've still been in the front row, bouncing to the beat as the crowd recited every word. Classic hip-hop was more my speed, but the blaring music and frenetic energy of their performance won me over.

After an opening by a girl-group I'd likely never hear from again, the show started with a high-energy set from their newest recruits and continued with performances by the rest of the camp. I was on the verge of restless when Vince burst onto the stage to perform with the headliner, Too Much. A scream bubble up my chest, but I clapped a hand over my mouth before it could escape.

Clad in all black, he handled the stage like a pro. I couldn't take my eyes off of him and neither could the rest of the women surrounding us. When their song concluded, the rapper introduced Vince in his signature southern drawl, and left him to perform the lead-single from the soundtrack of his upcoming movie.

Vince started his song, a mid-tempo groove about the ups and downs of love. His voice was a perfect blend of honey and smoke, and had me ready to give him everything I had. In that moment, I understood why women threw their underwear on stage. I'd never throw mine, but I wanted to throw *something*.

He finished his set to thunderous applause. As he exited stage left, I wondered what it would be like to be the woman that greeted him after every performance or at least the woman he wrote all his songs about.

When we arrived backstage, I had the feeling they'd extended passes to everyone as there was hardly room to turn around. It was ok, though, we clung to each other's backs as if we were in the club.

"That booty was definitely on credit," Amara said, staring as the crowd parted ways for the group's female rapper to walk through.

"Why are you looking in the first place?" Nina asked.

"Umm, isn't everyone?"

"Yes!" we said, together.

I laughed along, but my mind was elsewhere. I kept hearing Vince's voice in my head, calling me to his side like the pied piper. My heart wanted to follow, but the prospect of suffering the same fate as those mice helped me remain cautious.

"Hey, Sashimi. Why are you so quiet?" Amara asked, nudging my arm.

"Hu-what? Oh, no reason," I smiled and rejoined the conversation. "Come on. I need to find Vince, but I'm not sure that will happen with all these people around."

"I can find him!" Amara said.

"No!" Both Nina and I shouted together. It would likely involve someone being cursed out or threatened.

"I'll handle this," Nina said.

We watched as she sauntered her way through the mob and up to the nearest bodyguard in sight. It was seconds before she had him drooling. I shook my head and laughed, feeling sorry for all the men who'd fallen prey to her charms.

"Easy as pie," she said, motioning for us to follow her. We pushed through and continued down the main hallway, turning right when it came to an end. This opened up to another hallway, but as it was guarded by another set of Incredible Hulk twins, it was less crowded.

"Hi guys," Nina said, raising her voice a few octaves.

For a minute, they stared as if they'd seen a new species for the first time. My laughter broke their trance though, and they quickly regained their composure.

"Name please," one of them said as he stole glances at her breasts.

"Oh," she giggled, "Vince said we could stop by."

Twin gazes traveled up and down her body, drinking in her long legs, full hips and breasts. She'd oiled all of the above into a dress that could've been her skin, if not for its sky-blue hue. Nina did a quick spin to give them the full effect. At this, the men parted ways and let us through without even a glance at myself or Amara.

"Well, damn, Sasha. We must be chopped chittlins," Amara said, reading my mind.

"I know!" I laughed. "Hold on, I need to stop for a second." I propped myself against the closest wall to step out of my shoes.

"I don't know why you insist on wearing shoes you can't walk in," Nina said.

"First of all, I can walk in them. They just hurt," I replied. "Secondly, they match my outfit perfectly." I motioned to the silk white tank top and gold, snakeskin-patterned pencil skirt. The ensemble was definitely more sexy than demure, but compared to the yard of chiffon Amara wore, it might as well have been a choir robe.

Nina shook her head and laughed. "Such pain in the name of love."

"Please, your shoes are higher than hers!" Amara pointed out.

"Yes dear, but you don't see me holding onto the wall for dear life, do you?"

I laughed and took a few more minutes to rest my feet. Now that the shoes were off, I noticed how stiff they were. An investment in ballet flats wouldn't be all that bad, but I hated feeling shorter than everyone else. That and they didn't make my legs look as good.

After returning the shoes to their rightful place, we continued down the corridor to see a smorgasbord of women, a handful of men, and my newest friend loitering near the dressing rooms. Martinique had a style. Not style in the sense of elegance or sophistication, but "a style"— a go-to look that required little imagination and even less fabric. The dress wasn't latex this time, but it still clung to her curves like glue.

"I should've known," I said

"What?" Nina stopped mid-stride.

I motioned toward Martinique and her clan of groupies.

"Who is that?" she asked.

"The girl I told you about, from the set."

"Please don't tell me I'm going to have to use my blade," Amara said, rifling through her purse.

"How did you—nevermind."

"Guys, let's just—" I stopped when Vince emerged from the dressing room. The women surrounded him like a flock of seagulls on a fish. He greeted them all then slid an arm around Martinique's waist, making it obvious there was more to their relationship than just video shoots.

"What the hell?"

"It's cool," I said, despite the fire simmering in the pit of my stomach.

"Cool? How the hell does he invite you somewhere then walk around with...with—" For once, she couldn't come up with a scathing remark.

"It's not like he invited me on a date or something."

"I don't know," Nina said. "This still doesn't feel right."

No, it didn't feel right, but what was I supposed to do? Had I really pulled the classic misread of signals? He said he'd wanted to see me, but did that have to mean something else? Had I *added* meaning where there was none? No. It was the typical male pattern bullshit. Sure, it was dressed up in a prettier package than usual, but it was all the same. Men were all the same.

"Let's just get out of—"

"Sasha?"

My traitorous legs quivered at the sound of my name on his lips and glued me to the spot. With purposeful, long-legged strides, he was at my side in no time.

"What's up? I didn't think you were coming."

"Obviously," Amara said.

"Yeah, I umm, I just decided to come on a whim."

"Cool. So, did you enjoy the show?"

"Nah uh, are you really about to act like you weren't just hugged up on that skank?" Amara said. I tried to shush her, but it was clear from the expression on Martinique's face that she'd heard.

"Excuse me!" she said, inching towards us.

"You're excused," Amara continued. "The exit is down the hall and to the left."

"OK, that's it. Let's go," I said, pulling her arm and leading her toward the exit she'd mentioned.

"Who the hell do you think you are?" someone called out behind us.

"You can find out!" Amara reached into her purse, but Nina stayed her hand.

"Please don't do this here. Do you not see all those cell phones aimed at us?"

I hadn't noticed them myself, but when I took the time to focus on the crowd, at least five people had their phones raised. *Great!* A record round of fundraising nullified by petty foolishness.

"Come on," I shoved Amara away with Nina's help.

"Sasha, hold on," Vince caught up. "Don't pay them any mind. I don't."

"I can't tell," Amara said.

"Enough, ok! Can you guys excuse us for a moment?" I asked.

"Fine, but we're not leaving," Amara said, as they stood near the exit door and waited.

I turned to Vince, "Thanks for the invite, the show was great, but I think it might have been a mistake to come here."

"What? No, wait, I'm sorry about that—about her."

"It's ok. I didn't know you two had a thing."

"Nah, it's not that. She's just—"

"No need to explain," I cut him off. "It's none of my business."

It was easy to determine their situation. She was likely one of his "friends with benefits" and I had no interest in being the next beneficiary.

"Thanks again though. I'll...see you."

"Wait," he caught me by the waist, like he'd done minutes before to Martinique. I should have squirmed from his grasp, but the pin pricks of pleasure shooting through my body felt to good.

"Look, she really is just a friend. I've done tons of videos with her and that's it."

"Is that how you are with all your *friends*?"

"If by that you mean *comfortable*, then yes, I am. Does that bother you?"

Hell yeah, my mind screamed, but I crossed my arms and shook my head, no.

He smiled. "I'm having an after-party at my place. You should come."

It was an enticing offer, made more so by those dark, brooding eyes and full lips. Still, it was in my best interest to end things here. Being courted by Vince Parker was flattering, but the reality was I'd always be on defense and I wasn't interested in playing games.

"No thanks," I said. "I've had enough groupie UFC for one night. This was fun though."

"Ok, why does it feel like I'm getting the brush off?"

I shrugged out of his arms and headed towards my friends by the exit sign. Better to get out while I could still see it.

The morning sun crept through the drapes on tiptoe, leaving the bedroom drenched in a halo of light. Startled from a deep sleep by an unknown force, I glanced around half expecting someone to be in the room. Instead, there was only me, and a slightly menacing dress form tucked in the corner. The steady hum of the ceiling fan stirred across my face and tried to lull me back to sleep, but it was no use. I grabbed my phone and checked the time: 8:45am. That number couldn't be right. I blinked a few times, sat up on my elbow and pulled it closer to my face.

"Damn," I sighed but made no move to get up.

Thanks to my well-meaning friends, the majority of my weekend was now a blur of sleep, clubs and alcohol, so much so that I was sure I'd pee champagne when I finally made it to the bathroom. That was the problem with drinking. It was all fun and games until you woke up feeling like the Road Runner dropped and anvil on your head.

The icy, tiled floor of the bathroom woke me a bit more but did nothing for the dull ache that steadily pushed itself to my forehead. I peeled off my night-shirt and stared at my favorite claw-foot tub, wishing I had time for a bubble-bath. Instead, I stepped into the shower and relaxed against the wall while the warm water eased the tension out of my muscles.

Two days had passed since seeing Vince at the concert, but I still couldn't shake the disappointment of seeing him with Martinique. Couldn't shake the disappointment of knowing my instincts were correct. Oh well. It was fun while it lasted it.

By the time I shuffled in to work it was nearly 10am. Luckily, there were no meetings on the schedule until—

"Well, well! It seems we have a celebrity in our midst!"

I jumped and glanced up at London, a folder clutched to her chest as I waited in the bank of elevators. I couldn't remember getting *inside* the elevator. I didn't even remember getting out of the car. I shook my brain free and headed for the office.

"What's up?"

"Well, there's this blogger named Nicky Vicky and she—"

"Did you see this?" Nina burst into the room before I had the chance to hang up my coat.

"Well, damn. Does everyone in this office shirk proper greetings?"

"Nevermind that," she held her tablet up to my face. "Do you see this?"

I took extra time to put my things away then snatched it from her. "*Groupies Going at It!*" the title of the video promised. I didn't have to press play to know what I'd see. I did anyway and watched the replay of Martinique and Amara's confrontation: 300,000 views and counting.

"That's not all," Nina said, pulling up some random blog. I never realized how quickly these people worked. It disturbed me to think of the sleep they lost for the sake of articles that were 95% conjecture. The only true statement was in regard to my run-in with Martinique, though calling it a stand-off was a bit much. Besides, Martinique was probably the "anonymous" party who'd given them the information. Anything to stay relevant, I guess.

"No big deal," I handed it back to Nina.

"Oh no?" She took it, swiped her fingers across the screen and gave it back. "What about that?"

This time it was Martinique's Twitter page:

@sashelle: Some woman just don't know when to step off!
#THIRSTY

"Truthfully, I don't know which makes me more upset, the reference to me or her poor grammar."

"I can't believe she has the nerve to follow you," London said.

All of this confirmed I'd made the right choice in ending whatever I'd started with Vince. I had enough issues to deal with. No need to add nosy paparazzi and crazy groupies.

"Anyway, we don't have time for this right now," I checked my watch. "We have a conference call in five minutes and a pro—"

The door swung open and Amara stepped inside carrying several shopping bags.

"Hey ladies! Where's the fire?"

"What is this, Grand Central? What are you doing here? Doesn't your new job start today?" I asked.

"Nina didn't tell you?"

"Tell me what?"

"Ooh, umm, London come help me uh…just come on."

She pulled the confused assistant out the door.

"Tell me what?" I called after her.

"She said I could work here for a bit, sort of like an intern."

"She said you—God, I don't have time for this." I marched past her and headed for the door.

"Oh, come on, Sashimi. You're always telling me to get a job so…"

"Yeah, but I never mentioned getting one here. Ever."

I loved the girl, but I didn't need a crystal ball to tell me no good would come from allowing her to work at Sashelle. To my knowledge, she'd never held a job for longer than a month and if she had, the probability that she'd done actually work was slim to none. I turned around to grab my messenger bag and phone, which vibrated when I swiped it from the desk.

"So…is that a yes?"

"Absolutely not. Besides, you said you were going back to school."

"Maybe next year."

"You said that last year."

"Well, stuff came up."

"Exactly. And if I let you work here, that same stuff is going to

40

get you the boot and likely ruin our friendship. Now," I placed a hand on her back and guided her towards the door. "Take this stuff and run along."

"Fine. There was something in here for you, but I guess I better *run along*," she stuck out her tongue and walked out.

"I don't take bribes," I called after her.

My belongings made a dull thud when I tossed them on the floor after entering my apartment. I kicked my shoes against the nearest wall and headed straight for the bathroom. After a day of juggling design issues and convincing my brain that reading blogs wasn't a good idea, only a shower could resuscitate my drained mental state.

After standing under its warm jets for much longer that I should have, I readied myself for bed. In my room I set the alarm, turned on the radio and slid beneath the comforter as the soothing sounds of soft jazz filled the room. My lids were heavy, but instead of sleep it was thoughts of Vince that settled into my mind. How could he be such a jerk, I wondered. Going on and on about wanting to see me only to jump on the next train moving when I arrived late. I kept trying to tell myself it didn't matter. All day I'd used the video as exhibit A in my case against him, but I couldn't be convinced of his guilt.

"Ah!" I kicked the sheets and turned over.

Determined to erase all traces of him, I concentrated on other things: bunnies, rainbows, and a nice piece of silk-satin. Anything to keep my brain occupied until sleep swept— I jerked at the blaring sound of my phone. The clock read 2:10am, but that couldn't be right. There was no way I'd been up musing about him for over three hours. Better still, who in the world had the nerve to call so late? I checked the screen: private number? Decline.

I tossed the phone onto the extra pillow and slid back under the covers. No sooner had I closed my eyes than the phone rang again. I snatched it up and accepted the call:

"Something better be on fire because if it isn't, you will be— whoever you are!"

"Now is that any way for a lady to speak?" said a voice I hadn't heard in days.

I sat up straighter and smoothed my hair as if he could see me.

"It's 2am. I am not concerned about being a lady. Who is this?"

The attitude I tried to infuse quickly dissipated.

"Damn. Are there so many men calling that you can't figure it out?"

"Maybe."

He laughed, though it came across more like a groan of pleasure.

"Wait a minute. How did you get my cell number?"

"I talked your friend into giving it to me—the bald one."

Of course. Amara would've cut off *his* finger before giving it to him.

"Right so..."

"I would've called sooner, but I'm on location and this is the first free moment I've had. I feel like I owe you an explanation."

"You don't. You really don't. I'm flattered by the *interest* you've taken in me, but let's just call this what it is and move on."

"I don't know what you mean."

"It means I'm not interested in becoming your side chick or your main chick or— whatever so...yeah, good luck with your music and good night or good morning or...whatever."

I ended the call and slammed the phone atop the night stand. With the verdict rendered, I tried again to go back to sleep and hoped I didn't regret it later.

Chapter 5

I looked like a raccoon. Well, that might have overstated it, but with the dark circles under my eyes I definitely resembled a sleep-deprived vampire or hungry zombie. I applied a few more layers of concealer then snapped the compact closed.

It was Vince's fault. After hanging up on him, I tried going back to sleep, but every time it was within my grasp, it slipped away like an eel. Several espresso shots kept the sleepiness at bay but did nothing for the physical manifestations. Luckily, a day of sketching and adjusting samples was complete, freeing me to squeeze in a class of yoga.

"London," I said, pushing the intercom.

"Ne, sangjung— err, yes ma'am."

"Is there anything left on the schedule?"

"Jana rescheduled, so there's—"

"Umm, hello? Why aren't you ready yet?" Nina rushed through the door, coat in hand.

"What are you talking about?"

"Oh, my gosh," she ran a hand over her head. "The charity event. How could you forget? I told you about this weeks ago."

"That was your first mistake. You know you should have told London."

"Are you totally incapable of remembering things on our own?"

"Not when I want to remember them." I stood up and grabbed my coat as well.

"I already sent the RSVP and it would be rude not to show up. Especially when we'll likely need Arisa's fundraising skills at some point."

I sighed. She was right. I hated when she was right.

"Do I have to change?" I gestured to the billowy black Kaftan.

"That's fine," she waved me off. "Men like that 'hide and seek' look."

"Shut up!"

A throng of 20-somethings bustled to life as Nina and I approached the entrance of 48nyc. Their smart phones locked onto us, ready to capture the next hashtag. Unfortunately for them, we weren't A-list material and their focus returned to a fresh round of selfies.

"Umm, I don't know about you, but nothing about this crowd or line has my name on it."

"Oh, come on, Sashimi. Have a little faith," Nina said, strutting past the crowd and up to Arisa—a petite woman with spiked blond, hair controlling the front. If the gathering of people grew unruly, I wasn't sure how her 90lbs. of skin and bone would fend them off. Then again, with the man who resembled a bear on its hind legs standing at the door, she'd be fine.

"Nina, hi! I'm so glad you could make it," she said, to the dismay of those next in line. She gave Nina a quick hug then scrolled through her clipboard to mark off a name. "We're starting the speed date in a few so hurry inside."

"Speed date—wait a minute!" I grabbed Nina's arm. "Did you know about this?"

"Umm, no?" she swatted me away. "But since we're here, use this opportunity to get over that cracked heart. I'm sure you'll find some yummy fish to reel in."

I didn't know which annoyed me more, her blind optimism or her corny turn-of-phrase. There wasn't much I could do, so I followed her inside.

In a place like Manhattan, three things were inevitable for a single woman:

1. She'd run into her ex at the most random of places.

2. She'd be "hooked up" on a number of blind dates.

3. Her sometimes irritating, but well-meaning friends would drag her to a public venue in hopes of meeting a rebound.

For these reasons I made it a rule to overdress whenever we went out. Yet the one time I broke the standard, Nina dragged me into what was clearly a semi-formal event—judging by the many women wearing cocktail dresses.

Under normal circumstances, I wouldn't care that my outfit didn't fit some theme, but the fact that I'd been conned into the situation left me uncomfortable.

Still, with the combination of Sade's mellow vocals and the lounge's calming tones of purple, grey and beige, my annoyance began to dissipate.

"Come on." Nina pulled me towards a table by the closest window.

44

"Umm, what is this?" I asked, grabbing a red and white, "Hello, my name is…" sticker.

"Just write your name, ok."

The sugary smile she'd included with her directive should've been a warning. Instead of following my instincts, I complied with her request and wrote my name… then balled it up. There was a huge stack of tags, so I grabbed another one and started over. Once finished, I turned to Nina and stuck the tag to the front of my dress.

"Mei Ling?" She read the tag. "You're too much."

"Hey, might as well have some fun, right?"

As we turned to search for seats, the number of patrons in the lounge surprised me. Based on the crowd gathered outside, I thought the venue would be full. Thankfully, there were just enough people to move through the space comfortably.

Nina pointed to an empty sectional near the back and we hurried to sit just as Arisa stepped up to a podium by the bar.

"Hello everyone and thank you for participating in our first annual Celebrity Speed Date."

"Seriously? How did you even get us in here?" I glared at Nina who pretended to be engrossed in the rules for the proceedings. I should've paid attention too, but my focus shifted to the people in attendance. Amongst the regular folks were celebrities—though they were more of the B and C-list variety—casually drinking and laughing.

"Hey, you ready?"

An elbow pierced my side and I turned to Nina's expectant grin.

"You know you're going to burn for this, right?"

"Ugh, stop being so dramatic and just have fun. It's starting!" She rubbed her hands together like some scheming villain.

"Ok, but do you speed date sitting on a couch? Aren't there supposed to be tables and chairs and whatnot?" I motioned to the cushy beige sectionals lining the walls.

"Weren't you listening? Their starting with groups of 12. The ladies will sit while the men rotate in those armless chairs in front of us." She stopped to grab a sheet of paper from a frosted glass table to our left then held it up. "You keep notes on these. If the guy you like likes you too, they'll hook you guys up with each other's info at the end."

It was simple enough, but the addition of famous men had me nervous. I prayed that my partners would be average. Several guys later, I prayed a different prayer: for time to speed up and rid me of the idiots sitting in front of me.

Question: How could four minutes feel like twenty?

Answer: When the person in front of you answers every question with a question thus never answering a question. That, or their own questions were inappropriate for someone they'd only known for five minutes.

So far I'd encountered one celebrity—an actor from the 90's looking to make a comeback. He was nice enough, but the shiny gold grill he wore distracted me from anything he had to say. The rest of the guys monopolized the time with scripted monologues about their "greatness".

"Time's up!" The pixie-voiced organizer yelled while shaking a bronze cowbell.

"Oh, thank God!" I mumbled loud enough for the current "date"—a broker with halitosis—to hear. Without offering a second glance, I fished my phone from my purse. Five missed calls from Amara, the screen blinked. I sent a text: *still here. Come at your own risk!*

"Is that Amara? Tell her to get her ass over here," Nina nudged my arm.

"Why subject another innocent soul to such cruelty?"

"Oh stop, it's not that bad."

"Please, being shot is the only thing that would make it worse."

"Whatever," she said, turning to the new candidate across from her.

Giggling, I tossed the phone back in my purse and rummaged around for a piece of gum. As usual, it was nowhere to be found. I considered turning the bag upside down until I heard the chair in front of me being pulled out. It was rude to continue the search, but I really wanted that gum.

"Hey, what's up?"

My scalp tingled at the sound of an unfamiliar baritone. The rest of my body followed suit when a broad chested, snack of a man slid into the seat. Whether it was the one dimple in his right cheek, or the heady scent of his cologne I couldn't say; one of them had me leaning forward in anticipation. The closer I got though, the more I recognized who he was.

"Hey, what a minute. Aren't you—"

"Yeah, I *was*," he interrupted, "it's just C Sharp now."

"Uh ok," I nodded.

He'd changed his name, but I was certain it wouldn't do much good. The one or two hits he'd had back in the day were off the coattails of another, more popular, rapper from his city.

"So, what brings—"

"Yo, I think I know you." He squinted at my name tag, frowned, looked at it again. "M-My Ling? That's yo' name? I coulda sworn it was something else."

He snapped his fingers.

"Sasha! It's Sasha, right?"

"Umm, yeah," I hesitated, "How did you know?"

"You Vince's girl."

"Uh, I don't think—"

"Yo, you gotta check this out."

I rolled my eyes. Not only did he cut me off at every sentence, now he had the nerve to hand me some headphones.

"Listen to this."

"Umm, I am not putting those in my ear."

"Oh, aight." He detached the cord from his phone and played what I assumed to be a track from his "long awaited" comeback, without bothering to lower the volume. His rap skills were never that great to start, and time hadn't done much to improve them. If anything, his attempt at the mumble rap trend only made it worse. Still, he bopped along as if it was the best thing he'd ever heard.

"So whachu think? It's dope, right?"

"Umm, I uh—"

"Hey, you think you could have Vince listen to this?"

"Yeah, umm, I really don't know him like that," I said, returning to the gum search in my bag.

"Don't know who like what?"

This new voice wasn't new at all. In fact, it was one I was sure I'd never forget. Vince stood behind Mr. Awful Rapper, wearing a black and blue, color-blocked sweater and a mischievous smile.

"Ayy, Vince Parker! What up, man?" the artist now known as C Sharp said, standing to offer Vince a hand.

"What's—oh shit—is that you Ch—"

"Nah, it's C Sharp now—yeah, you know, I'm *rebranding.*"

Rebrand your ass up out this seat!

"Oh ok, well, good luck with that," Vince said, trying to step around.

"Thanks man, oh wait, you gotta listen to this. I just let ya girl hear it and she said it was dope.

I shook out a quick "no" when Vince looked to me for confirmation.

"Umm, yeah, send it to me on IG or "at" me or something."

"Aight, cool, cool," he stepped back and let Vince take the seat then realized that left him without one. He glanced around for a moment then decided to leave. I laughed as he bopped his way out the door. I turned my attention back to Vince, who now sat appraising me. He leaned forward.

"Hi. I'm Vince Parker. Nice to meet you—", he squinted to read the sticker, "Mei?"

Just like that, my brain took a leave of absence. Thankfully, the smile and nod sequence was still intact. I did both and willed my mind to return. It didn't work. It couldn't when his presence alone held me captive.

I closed my eyes to free the chains and when I opened them, I saw that he'd extended his hand to me. I obliged. He brushed his lips across the back then kissed it softly. A slow fire ignited in my chest and singed everything I'd said on the phone.

"Umm, nice to meet you again."

"So, what's a girl like you doing in a place like this, Mei?" He asked, a hint of smile playing at his lips.

"Please, call me Sasha."

I suddenly wanted my name on those lips.

"Sasha, huh. I like it." He laughed—a deep vibration that was more a groan of pleasure. *I* liked it.

"And to answer your question, I was dragged here by my well-meaning yet totally over-bearing, best friend," I said, though she pretended not to hear.

"Remind me to thank her later," he leaned forward. "So, tell me, what do I have to do to get you to take me seriously?"

"Umm…"

"You've been brushing me off like you're not interested in—"

"I wasn't interested."

He leaned closer though I didn't think it possible.

"Wasn't? Does that mean you're interested now?"

"Maybe." I leaned away.

"What changed?"

I searched for an answer but couldn't find one that made sense. Just last night I'd told him to take a hike and now? Now with him sitting in front of me, the epitome of sexy in that cashmere sweater, jeans, and boots, I knew I wanted him. Forget the inevitable crash and burn, I wanted him.

I couldn't tell him that though. Not for it to be thrown back in my face at some later date. No, I'd keep it to myself and at least save face if all his attention turned out to be a strategy to divide and conquer.

"Sasha," he said, grabbing both my hands.

I sucked in a breath and bit my bottom lip. *So, this is what his hands feel like.*

By now we were close enough to kiss, not that I wanted to. Well…anyway, I breathed deep to clear my thoughts then tried to release his hands. Vince held tighter.

"Am I making you uncomfortable?"

"Err, just a tad."

He nodded but made no effort to release me. "You'll get used to it."

Will I? The better question was "could I"? Could I allow myself to let go of my hang ups and give this a chance? Was it worth risking my heart yet again only to have it handed back to me? I didn't know.

"Alright, well," I said, standing before things got out of hand. "It was great seeing you again, but I should probably get out of here."

I tried for a quick escape but tripped on Nina's outstretched foot. Before I could catch myself, his arm draped around my waist.

"Why are you always trying to get away from me?" He brushed a strand of hair from my face. This guy definitely had an issue with boundaries, though it was becoming harder to argue with them. I glanced around and noticed that nearly everyone was watching us. We'd received casual glances before, but now they were outright staring.

"I'm not trying to get away," I stepped out of his grasp. "It's just late and I have some business-related things to—"

"It's your business, right? That means you can put whatever you need to do off, at least for a little while."

"I could put it off, yes, but we—" I looked to Nina for back up, but she'd disappeared. After a cursory glance, I found her at the bar surrounded by several men. Good. That meant I could sneak out.

"Wait, wait." He caught me by the waist. "Are you free now? Grab some dinner with me."

"I already ate but thank you."

I could tell he wanted to say more, but he bit his lip and smiled. I wished I was that lip. *Damn it!*

"I'll call you later then, if that's ok."

Was it ok? From what I'd seen so far, this road could only end with me at another bar, disillusioned.

"I don't know if that's a good idea. I just got out of a—thing and I want to lay low for a while." *You'll probably be worse than him,* is what I really wanted to say.

This time when I tried to leave, he simply took my hand and placed it between his. The warmth of his palms climbed up my arms and into my chest, gradually melting my resolve.

"I understand that. I can take it slow."

Clearly, I wasn't going to win this battle, especially when I wasn't that interested in fighting. Especially when he wasn't playing fair. Common sense knew what to do. It was just too bad it walked out with "no chance" the rapper.

"OK," I gave in. "Call me later."

Chapter 6

When the car service dropped me at a building nestled between two SoHo retail stores, I thought we'd be shopping until I pushed through the doors and found myself in the modern lounge of a recording studio.

Photos of what I guessed were previous clients lined the walls, along with artists renditions of famous musicians. I approached the brick and granite desk where a youngish man with large, wire-rimmed glasses sat staring at a computer.

"Hi, umm. I'm here to see Vince Parker."

"Alright, I just need to see some identification."

My brow wrinkled, but I passed him my ID anyway.

"Sorry," he said. "It's just a precaution. People come in here all the time trying to get into the studios to meet artist. So, we ask them to make a list with us of who might be showing up."

"Understood," I said, returning the card to my purse.

"Take the elevator to the third floor and room A will be just to the left."

I followed his instructions and on the third floor, pushed through a door marked "A" and into a blue-lit studio. Just behind the door was a large sectional occupied by three girls, all of whom gave me a once over when I stepped inside. There were a few guys standing around, but their reaction was opposite. Where the women offered barely concealed scowls, the men smiled openly, and one even gave up his seat at the table in the center of the room.

"Play that back," Vince's voice rose from the speakers. I could only see his outline as he stood at the microphone behind a wall of glass.

As I wondered how to get his attention without disrupting the proceedings, movement registered in my peripheral vision. I readied myself for another verbal altercation but found a fair-skinned man of medium build and thinning hair standing at my side. He was shorter than the rest and wore an Italian suit with a polka-dot bowtie.

"Hello," he said, resting against the table. "You here for Vince?"

My gaze flickered to the other women on the couch. They watched expectantly.

"Hello, and yes, I am."

"Interesting."

"Interesting how?" I ventured.

"Well, he doesn't usually bring anyone in here."

"Then these other people are..."

"Oh, producers, friends and that one is a *cousin,*" he said, pointing to a short, bald guy with caramel skin and gauges in his ears.

"So, how long have you guys been seeing each other?"

"Seeing—no it's not like that. We're...friends," I answered, but it didn't feel like the right word. Maybe I didn't want it to be the right word. He nodded though he didn't seem to buy the story either.

"So where did—"

"Ok, Carter, that's enough." Vince stepped out of the booth. A smirk eased on to his face as he crossed the room and pulled me up for a hug. Everyone stilled, and I was reminded of that old cliché' about silence and pins dropping and what not. Maybe there was some truth to short man's words.

I pulled out of his embrace and stepped back.

"Hey," he said.

"Hi."

I fiddled with the tassel on my purse to keep from looking into his eyes—dangerous territory. We stood like that for a moment: the others watching him, him watching me, me watching my purse.

"Right, so, give me a second to wrap up here then we can go."

"Go? Go where. I thought this was it."

"Nope. It's a surprise."

I tried to quell my nerves as we entered the back of his black sedan a few minutes later. The white leather seats felt like silk beneath my fingertips. I'd been in nice cars before, but this... it wasn't a car; more like a mobile, luxury apartment. I stretched my legs and leaned back with a sigh.

"Like it?" Vince asked.

"Mhmm."

"Try this." He pushed a button on the center console, setting off the vibrations of a gentle massage.

"You know I'm never getting out of here, right?"

"Fine by me," he said.

The driver started the ignition and the melodious voice of Carl Thomas surrounded us. Had someone given this guy my playbook? If so, I didn't care. I closed my eyes and tried to commit the moment to memory: beautiful car, beautiful music, beautiful man at my side. What could be better?

"So, what did you think?" he asked.

"Hmm?" I glanced up to find him staring intently.

"What did you think of the song?"

How to put it?

"It was…nice."

"That bad, huh?" he laughed.

"No, it wasn't bad. Just—something was missing. It felt like you were holding back."

"Holding what?"

"I don't know, exactly. Its— I heard the words, but it didn't seem like you believed them. Don't get me wrong, your voice is…wow, but that feeling, that longing just wasn't there. You know—" I turned and found him staring out the window. *Crap!* I must have gone too far. Well, he'd asked for an honest opinion. *Yeah, but you could have added some agave syrup or something.*

"I'm sorry, Vince. I didn't—"

"Why are you apologizing?" He finally looked at me, though not with the anger I thought I'd find. No, it was something else entirely. A look that stole my breath, stole my thoughts.

"Umm…" was all I could muster.

He leaned over the console between us, not helping the situation.

"You okay?"

"Uh, yes." I cleared my throat and fiddled with the collar on my jacket.

"Good, now why the apology?"

"I thought you were upset."

"Upset, no. More like surprised."

"Surprised?"

"Mhmm," he looked over my shoulder and smiled. "We're here, though I might have wasted a trip."

"Huh?"

"Nothing. Come on," he said, exiting the vehicle. I followed him onto the sidewalk and furrowed my brows at one of the city's most popular museums.

"Hmm, I never pegged you for an art buff."

"Hey, what can I say? I'm a sucker for beautiful things," he said, smiling down at me.

"Cornball," I coughed out.

"What was that?"

"Oh nothing. So, you come here often?"

"Yeah. They have an Emerging Artist showcase once a month. I like to show support when I can."

I stared at him for a moment before shaking myself out of it.

"What?" he asked.

"Nothing, you're just…not how I expected you to be."

Vince frowned. "I don't know whether to be flattered or offended.

"Let's go with flattered."

I patted his arm and we continued through the quiet corridors. Vince observed each exhibit with a new intensity and I noted how different he was from the character's he portrayed in film. Then again, maybe this was a character too.

Like most negative thoughts, it began to nag a small part of my brain until I found myself closing down.

"What do you think of that?"

"Huh?"

"In the case. What do you think?"

Something behind his smile made me curious as he pointed towards a large glass case. I stepped forward, nervous at what I might find inside.

My face wrinkled in confusion at the contents. There were two books, if they could be called that. One was open to a page of the color black and a page of cream. The second book had been opened to a pastel blue page and a lighter blue on the opposing side. The pages had no texture, nothing to give them an extra oomph.

"They're kidding, right?" I asked Vince, who grinned and shook his head, no.

I turned back towards the case, baffled as to what was to be obtained from a photograph of the color black; an ashy black at that. Perhaps it was the simplicity that was supposed to arouse the senses. Or maybe it was the contrast of the colors that made it important. In any case, I crossed my arms and smirked at the display case before turning away.

"What?" Vince chuckled, interlocking our arms. I offered him a timid smile, still unnerved by his affection.

"It's a book of colored pages. What am I supposed to do with that?" I tried not to laugh and failed.

"Come on, Sasha. It's not that bad."

"So, you say!"

We continued along with Vince steering me towards works he found of interest. I tried to ooh and aah in the proper places. Mostly

I just stared at him and wondered why he wasn't propped up on one of the walls. When he paused, I looked away and focused on a painting that resembled splatters of ink.

"OK, I can't take it anymore," Vince whispered after a few minutes of silence. "What in the world are you thinking?"

"Very Jackson Pollock-ish," I said.

"You know Jackson Pollock?" His brow lifted in surprise.

"Why wouldn't I?"

"OK, OK. Good." He rubbed his hands together. "So, what do you think of this one?"

"You want the truth?"

"It always sets you free."

I laughed at the sorry excuse for a joke.

"Well, the truth is, I just...don't get it," I began. "That's weird coming from a designer, I know. I should be able to see the art in everything, right?"

He shrugged his shoulders and nodded.

"While I do see its merit—its pattern would be great on a skirt—I'm wondering what makes this art. Is it because he sprinkled paint around in a haphazard manner?"

"Possibly."

Humor colored his voice as he answered, but I ignored it and continued what was fast becoming a rant.

"I mean, I understand at the time this style was created it was unlike anything else, but does that make it good? Biking shorts were the style at one point, but that didn't mean they were good."

"Wait, aren't they making a comeback?"

"Don't remind me," I said, rolling my eyes.

Vince laughed. "Ok, I get your point, but the fact that we're having this conversation is exactly what makes art good. Its success comes from the discussion it creates."

I twisted my head to study him. In return, he took my hand, kissed it then gently caressed the inside of my elbow. Heat rose to my cheeks and I quickly searched for something to take my attention off my ever-increasing body temperature.

"Hey, wait a minute. Why are we the only people here?" How had it taken me that long to notice?

"Oh, they're getting ready for one of the exhibits I mentioned and are closed to the public."

"We're the public." I motioned between us.

"Yeah, well, anyway. I'm a patron here so I asked them to make an exception."

I wasn't sure how to answer that, so I gave a quick nod, and let him continue to guide me through various rooms. Vince knew bits of information about nearly every piece we came across. That either meant he was truly the art buff he claimed to be, or he'd memorized a ton of facts for the sake of impressing me. My ego chose the latter though I quickly reminded it that we probably weren't the first to receive this treatment. The thought made my head hurt so I focused instead on the little white blocks near all the paintings on the wall. They all contained the name and other biographical information of the work's creator. After reading a dozen or so, I realized most of the pieces were rendered by men. *Figures!*

"Hey, what's that?"

I turned to see Vince pointing toward a sectioned off area. It was clearly the museum's way of saying "keep out", but it didn't stop him from dragging me up to the red ropes.

"I think this is the stuff from the new artist," he whispered.

"I think they want us to stay out."

"Oh, come on, have a little fun."

Vince pulled me forward when I hesitated then guided me around the metal poles and deeper into the room. I should have protested, but the dopamine surging through my brain clouded every thought and sensation except his hands gripping my waist.

"Yo, this is kinda cool."

His voice called me back to the surface. For the first time, I paid attention to the small space we'd entered. It looked more like a construction zone than a potential art exhibit. Canvases of varying sizes lay in stacks around the room. Wire cables hung dangled from the ceiling like tentacles. The walls were bare except for a trio of photos hanging against the widest one in the back. I knew he'd want to get closer, so I didn't bother protesting when he pulled me forward. If I had, I might have seen the canvas sticking out just enough to trip me up.

"Ahh!" I cried, groping for Vince as my body pitched forward. He spun around just in time for me to face-plant into his chest.

"Sorry, I uh, lost my footing there."

I used his shoulders to steady myself though it might have been safer to have hit the floor. The taut muscles beneath my fingers brought flashbacks of bare skin at the video shoot. Knowing only a soft layer of cashmere stood in the way, left my mouth dry.

"Sasha?"

"Huh—umm yes?" I snatched my hands away and took a step back.

"I asked if you're ok."

"Oh, yeah," I faked a laugh, "I'm fine I just—"

Stopped.

The almost fall had forced us closer to the wall-mounted photos. Though the pictures were still a short distance away, I didn't need to get any closer.

"Sasha, what's—what's wrong?" Vince asked, glancing between me and the wall.

I didn't need to get any closer, yet my feet moved anyway.

"Did—did they tell you whose art would be up next?"

"Yeah, some guy named Dean Seymour or something. He sounds like an ass," Vince said, with a laugh.

"*Zamore*. Dean Zamore," I said to myself.

"Hey wait a minute!" Vince exclaimed, moving to stand beside me. He looked from the photo, to me and back. "Is that *you*?"

I nodded as we both stared at the woman propped against a deteriorating brick wall. Wet, obsidian hair snaked down her nude frame like a second skin. Her feet—clad in red Pointe shoes—pierced the concrete of a city sidewalk. The tragic, urban landscape behind her seemed even more so in her presence. A trail-mix of feelings slowly crept into my mind as my pulse rate pushed toward a gallop.

This was the problem with pictures. The moments they captured rarely lasted longer than the flash. And even if they did, it wasn't long before it all went to hell, leaving you with a lifelong reminder of the war zone that washed away the happiness. Seeing the picture was seeing all the hopes and dreams I'd had in the moment. A pain, long dormant, swelled in the pit of my stomach. I grabbed Vince's arm just as my legs gave way.

"What's wrong?" he asked, pulling me towards a makeshift bench near the front of the room.

"It's nothing. I'm fine, I umm, I need to go."

"Sasha, what's going on?" He glanced from me to the photo and back.

"Nothing, I just—I need some air. Can we get out of here?"

Before he could answer, a burst of adrenaline revived my limbs and pushed me towards the exit. I didn't know where it came from, but I was grateful as it propelled me from the ghost of relationships past.

Chapter 7

The phone wouldn't stop ringing. In my line of business, that could be a good thing. It wasn't. The calls weren't coming from buyers, or "It" girls begging for a dress to wear to their next engagement. I might've actually cheered had it been a warehouse or fabric producer calling with their latest set-back. But no, it was none of the above. My inbox and phone lines were being flooded by two-bit reporters looking to feed themselves off of Vince Parker's newest "relationship".

In a matter of days, I'd gone from being asked about my mini collection, to whether or not Vince and I were secretly engaged. How they'd come up with that was beyond me, though I had to acknowledge the way my breath faltered at the thought.

Tired as I was of the public's constant need for status updates on our relationship and continuous online speculation, I couldn't resist clicking through the link Amara sent, detailing our outing at the museum. After running out on Vince, I'd been demoted from "fling" to "heartbreaker" which I didn't think was such a bad thing. The article however, was a different story. It was too close to the truth for my comfort, and I wondered whether the museum director's willingness to close the facility had more to do with their need for extra publicity than Vince's patronage.

"Ugh, I don't have time for this." I slammed the laptop closed and studied the boards in the workroom again. We'd spent the last few hours fitting models and tacking up new photos, but I still wasn't convinced by the full lineup. Plus, Daniela had yet to show up which left me silently freaking out.

"There you are!"

I jumped at the sound of Nina's voice. How she managed to sneak up wearing 5" heels was either a testament to her stealth abilities or the sorry state of my hearing.

"Why are you hiding in here?"

"I'm not, I'm just reviewing some stuff."

"Good. We have time then."

She took a seat at the drafting table and crossed her legs.

"Are you ok?"

"Yes, for the 100th time, yes."

She nodded then flipped through a few swatches on the table.

She stopped on an orange, silk-wool blend. "You didn't order this, did you? It's hideous."

"Yes, I did, but that's not why you're here, so what's up."

"Capital Investment Group pulled out."

"What." I stopped mid-stride. "What happened?"

"They gave me the company line about being stretched too thin, but I'm sure the publicity has something to do with it. Bastards."

"But I don't understand. Tons of people are calling for orders *because* of the same publicity."

"I know, which is why I'm not worried...yet."

"Yet? What's that supposed to mean?" I crossed my arms.

"I don't want what's happening with you to affect us adversely. I mean, how serious are you about him? Are you willing to chance it?"

"Chance what? Why is everyone getting so worked up over nothing? He's cool and all, but we're just friends."

Even as I said the words, I wished they weren't true. I knew the risks of being involved with him, but the only ones that really concerned me were those related to my heart.

"Fine," Nina said. "You guys are just friends. So why did you run out?"

"I don't see what that has to do with—Daniela, hi!"

I smiled as the leggy modeled bustled in with a friend at her side. Thank God for interruptions. How could I tell her Dean was back? I had to do it sometime, but better to wait until we were in a private place with fewer things to throw. Then again, she'd be more likely to lecture me which might be just as bad.

"I'm so sorry I'm late. I had a meeting that ran a bit longer than expected," she said, tossing her bags on the floor. "Is it ok that my assistant is here?"

"No problem, I'm just—"

"I'll leave you guys to it," Nina interrupted. "I'll be back, and I want answers!"

"Whatever."

I sighed. Crisis averted, at least for the next 30 minutes or so. I took the chance to focus all my attention on getting the perfect fit for the garment.

"So, I hear you're dating Vince Parker," Daniela said.

"Ugh, not you too! Don't believe everything you hear—or read, for that matter."

"I know. These days' people are so eager to run with gossip just so they can be the first to post something and have it go viral.

"Exactly," I said, nipping the fabric at the waist.

"But seriously," she whispered. "You like him, right?"

"Umm…"

"Oh, come on. I won't say anything and besides, the public knows that much already."

"He's alright," I laughed. "But what about you? Date any cute guys—oh, keep this here," I instructed, giving her a fold of the dress to hold.

"Nah, not really. You know how it is with guys. I'm either too much for them or they're too much for me."

"Yeah right," her friend chimed in without looking up from her phone. "She's still hung up on her ex."

"Aren't we all?" I said.

We shared a laugh before I excused myself to grab a sample I'd left in the office. I was by the stairs when the "call of nature" forced my steps toward the restroom. Inside, I pondered the question of Vince Parker. Did I like him? Sure, but so did half the women in the country, and I wasn't willing to fight through any of them just to have my broken heart published in every magazine and gossip site.

"…you're taking me to Vince's party," a voice said as I prepared to exit the stall. I pulled the door closed and peeked through the crack to see Daniela refreshing her makeup.

"Sorry kiddo, no plus ones."

Party? Party? I shuffled the word through my mind. Ah yes, he'd mentioned a party to me, but I'd failed to commit the date to memory.

"God, this sucks. He's like, super-hot. I can't believe she's going out with him."

"Is she?" Daniela asked. "I didn't want to mention it to her, but he's always been a bit of a player."

"Which means?"

I moved closer to the split in the door when there was no answer. Knowing Daniela might "shoot her shot" was further proof that pursuing Vince would only lead to trouble. Still, knowing about the trouble meant I could at least prepare for it. Yeah, I could do that. I could play the game. Right?

When I stepped inside the top floor of the W Hotel, I wondered if I'd entered a party or the set of a Bollywood movie. Beautiful, jewel-toned draperies of Dupioni silk lined the walls, highlighted by a curved ceiling covered with lights.

I ran my hands along the fabric and talked myself out of snatching it down to make a dress. Intricately embroidered pillows lay scattered over bronze leather sectionals while lanterns of gold filigree dotted the room. Among these decorations, were artists creating live pieces on various mediums including canvases and naked bodies.

I'd seen more art in the last few weeks than in my life, but I was more concerned with the delicious smell of curry permeating the air. My stomach led the way to a buffet table filled with everything from kabobs and falafel to Baida roti and samosas. It was a fight, but I finally squeezed my arm through a gap of people to grab a piece of roti bread.

As I nibbled away, I couldn't shake the feeling that something was off. I glanced around at the bustling crowd then down at myself. There was no mistaking I was a bit over-dressed or maybe underdressed was a better way to describe the short, tan and nude Fendi dress that barely left anything to the imagination.

Either way, I was not *dressed* for what was obviously a Halloween party, a minor detail Vince had neglected to mention or maybe I'd neglected to listen. I would've asked what the proper attire was, but I was too excited about the prospect of being his date. Anyway, I looked good so shrugged it off and finished the last bite of the delicious, rustic bread.

The usual costume suspects were in play including sexy nurses, police, etc. but there were a few Sari wearers among the crowd. Had I known the party's theme, I would've worn one too and ended up learning the hard way that stilettos don't fare well with its many intricate folds. That was clear from the three women who nearly fell to their face when their heels got caught up in the fabric. I almost choked when I realized that one of those women was Jennifer Lawrence.

It was then that I took a moment to really focus on the faces in the crowd. Most of them were celebrities, though not all on the A-list.

It was easy to spot the rich and famous, but the same couldn't be said for Vince. Walking around to look for him was not an option, so I maneuvered my way to the open bar. This bartender didn't resemble MC Hammer, but he'd do. I was in the middle of ordering champagne when a firm hand settled around my waist.

"Hey ma." His warm breath tickled my neck.

I turned in his arms, "Sup pa."

"You know," he began, reaching out to wind a lock of my short hair in his fingers. "I thought you were going to stand me up."

I shrugged, "I was, but I had nothing else to do."

"Well, I'm glad your life is so dull." He laughed and pulled me in for a hug. The woodsy scent of his cologne filled my head. I drank it in as his hand gently massaged the small of my exposed back.

"Let's go outside," he motioned towards the covered terrace. I nodded, unable to form words. My brain was hazy as he led us through the glass doors and into the night air.

The view of NYC was breathtaking. Surprisingly, there wasn't much of a crowd as everyone seemed attracted to the music inside.

"So, what made you come tonight?"

"Umm, you invited me?" It came out more like a question than an answer.

He laughed, "I know that, but at the time it seemed like you were trying to get out of it."

A brisk wind swept through the terrace and left me shivering. Vince stood in front of me, gently rubbing my arms. He could have offered me his jacket, but I would've refused in favor of his hands, even if it they made it hard to concentrate.

A thin film of moisture rose from my palms. There was something in his expression that made me nervous. I'd seen eyes like them before. Dark, endless currents I'd lost myself in, many times before.

"So, tell me," he breathed against my cheek. "What *really* made you come here tonight?"

"You," I blurted without thinking. *So much for keeping it casual.*

"Mmm, why me?"

I didn't have a real answer, so I shrugged and tried to pull myself from his arms.

"Sasha, you don't have to be afraid of me. I'm not going to hurt you."

I tried to pop the laugh that bubbled to the surface, but it was impossible.

"What's so funny?" he stepped back, finally allowing some breathing room, though his hands remained on my arms.

"I'm sorry, it's just that, well, I wonder how many women have been in this exact same place. Your arms wrapped seductively around them while you whispered your undying affection to them."

It was hard to complete the thought without laughing as I

suddenly felt stuck in one of those corny romantic comedies.

He stared at me for a moment before dropping his arms from my body and turning to stand near the railing.

I watched his face as he stared into the clear night sky and suddenly, I felt like a complete idiot.

"Vince...I'm sorry. I didn't mean it like that." Ok, so the explanation was weak, but what else could I say?

"It's cool. I get it. You women are hilarious, though, always griping about wanting a man that's honest and when he is, you call him a liar." He paused for a moment to collect his thoughts.

"You know, that's probably why you're single," he turned to face me. "You don't know the difference."

That was a low-blow and I might have had a clever retort had I not been completely caught off guard by the comment. I opened my mouth to respond then shut it just as quickly.

"Tell me something. Do you really think I would go through so much trouble to get some? I mean, do I look like I have to go through so much trouble?" Vince gestured towards his perfectly formed body and I was pissed that I couldn't argue.

"Not to be rude or anything, but if that's what I wanted, there are plenty of women throwing themselves at me, everywhere I go."

I pinched my arm to keep my eyes from rolling. Stating the obvious wasn't going to help the situation, whether I agreed with him or not. Clearly, I had trust issues, and he being "Vince Parker" wasn't going to make it better. Which brought me back to the question of the century, was he worth the trouble?

"Sasha," he said, interrupting my thoughts. "I can admit my initial attraction to you was because you'd turned me down."

I knew it!

"But the more I saw you, the more I wanted you—even when I tried to deny it. We don't know each other that well, but I sensed you wanted the same. Was I wrong?"

What I sensed was a struggle taking place in my mind. Though I tried, it was hard to act as if he meant nothing. Every part of my body wanted to stake claim on him, yet my heart was afraid to take the risk.

Of course, it could all just be game; the cards he played on the rare occasion that a woman wasn't at his beck and call. But what if it were true? If he really meant what he'd said, what then?

"Vince..." I walked to his side slowly, allowing the right words to form.

"I can't believe I'm saying this but, you're right. I know I have trust issues, but you have to understand, it's so much harder with you who, as you say, has all these women throwing themselves at you daily. I don't know how I'm supposed to compete with that."

"Don't," he smiled, grabbing my hands. "None of them compare to you, Sasha."

"Vince, you don't even know me. I mean, we went on what, one date? Two?"

My mind was dizzy with the task of trying to keep up with what was happening and bringing memories back.

"I know that you're the most intriguing woman I've met in a while. And not only that, there's something about you that…I don't know what it is, but… I want it." His words were like honey, drizzling ever-so lightly over my bare skin. How could I believe him? How could I *not* believe him?

"Will you give me a chance?" He asked, sincerity burning through.

Afraid my voice would falter, I nodded.

"Ahh!" I yelled, when he swept me up in his arms and carried me back inside to the dance floor. Besides a few glances, no one paid much attention to us, which was just how I liked it.

"Dance with me," he said as a mellow groove flooded the room.

My feet were numb, but how could I care? I leaned back against his chest and closed my eyes as we grinded our bodies together like teenagers. Vince's hands slid over my arms as he placed soft kisses along my neck.

He kissed the crown of my head and I opened my eyes. I started to turn to him when a pair of dreadlocks caught my attention. It was a common hairstyle these days, but something about them seemed familiar. Even the body they were attached to…

"What's wrong?" Vince asked.

"Nothing, I…I think I see someone I uh, used to know." I'd already started walking in his direction. I couldn't stop myself…moth to a flame and all. I shook my head. In the dictionary, the picture next to the word cliché was one of us.

I wasn't sure how I made it from one side of the room to the other, but once I was close enough to reach out to him, I didn't know what to do. The people with him noticed me before he did, or maybe it was Vince who'd left their mouths agape. Either way, he turned to see what they were staring at. Dean's expression slackened and even over the music, I heard the spit he gulped down.

I'd rehearsed this moment a million times; the things I'd do when I saw him again: the haughty gaze. The Joan Collins-like slap. Feigned indifference. Imagination was cruel. Always made you believe you'd feel invincible in the moment. Now, I could only manage the basics. Breathe. Blink. Stare. Breathe. Blink. Stare.

"Sasha?"

Was it possible to cringe and swoon simultaneously? Thick muscled body wrapped in a knee-length blazer, and tapered slacks. A chiseled face that softened in just the right places. And eyes. The sultry eyes that always left me—no. I steeled my nerves and prepared to be the strong, silent type, but I wasn't fooling anyone. In five seconds, I'd be in tears.

I turned on my heels just as quickly as I'd come and pushed through the crowds toward the elevator.

"Sasha!"

Two voices called after me, but even the searing pain shooting through my feet wouldn't stop their retreat. I jammed the elevator button and the steel doors opened as if they'd been waiting for my return.

Chapter 8

Vince and I were official. At least that's what all the tabloids reported and since most people took their word for truth, the search to find out who I was and what I'd done to garner his attention was kicked up. They'd hounded me at my home and office until I'd had no choice but to hide out at the store-site in SoHo. Because I'd refused to answer their questions, they'd taken to creating stories of their own. Between their pages, I was everything from an opportunist seeking publicity for my company to his long-lost sister. Even Karen, my step-mom, questioned what was happening, after which I advised her to stop reading that garbage.

The phones in my office still rang off the hook. Buyers upping their orders and others who'd passed on the collection suddenly wanted every piece. We even had several stores request Sashelle capsule collections. All great developments, but I struggled with my feelings about it all. It was great to have new people interested in the company, but only time would tell if their interest was real or solely based on my new association with Vince.

My cell phone buzzed, jarring me back to the present. No name was assigned to the number glowing on the screen, but I didn't need one. Even after deleting those ten digits from my phone, they'd refused to vacate my brain.

Sasha? If this is you, can we have dinner? I need to see you…need to apologize.

I stared at the message, reading without comprehending. There was a time when I checked my phone every five minutes, hoping for anything from him. I was past that now, but I still couldn't stop myself from reading it again. This was exactly right. All my dreams were coming to fruition: the success of the line, the store opening weeks away. Years of hard work threatened by a nightmare named Dean dancing at the edges. Still, I couldn't let the text go unanswered…could I?

"Happy Birthday!"

I started at the sound of Nina's voice and turned to see her holding a bag from Momofuku milk bar.

"Ah, Crack pies, exactly what I needed."

In the madness of the last few days, I'd forgotten all about my birthday. If there was anything that could set my brain back on course, it was Crack pie: a gooey, buttery confection that made me sympathize with those addicted to the real stuff. We unwrapped the sweet treats and I laughed as Nina licked the powdered sugar they'd dusted over the top.

"God, this is like an edible orgasm," I mumbled through a mouthful. It would definitely be on the menu for my last meal.

"So, I know you told me you were fine, but how are you *really* feeling after the showdown at the W?"

"Is that what we're calling it?" I asked, taking another bite. The term fit, though I'd neglected to mention I'd fled the scene instead of facing him head-on.

"I'm feeling ok."

"Really?"

"No." I placed what was left of my pie back onto the wrapper. "I knew I wasn't completely over him, but I thought I was further along than this. I mean, my heart was in my throat when I saw him. How is that still possible after three years?"

"Old habits die hard."

"And Vince. I have no idea what to say. I feel so embarrassed right now."

"Just tell him the truth. It's not like you lied or were hiding something from him. Everyone has a past."

That fact should have reassured me, but it didn't. Whatever baggage Vince had, I was certain it didn't compare to a broken engagement.

"I'll think about it," I said.

"While you're at it, how about you reconsider letting Amara work for us."

"Ok, was this a birthday pie or a bribe pie?"

"Both?" she shrugged.

"Man, you know how that girl is. I love her, but she's super irresponsible and I don't want that to ruin our friendship."

"I hear that, but I think she has some ideas that could really help us."

"I'll think about it."

"You do that," she stood up. "I'm heading back to the office. See you at the house tonight."

I waved and watched her head out the service entrance. I'd yet to meet Dean, but already I felt like I'd betrayed her by not mentioning that I would.

For someone so eager to make amends, Dean was doing a poor

job of showing it. I'd waited for over twenty minutes and my patience was wearing thin. I stood ready to leave the restaurant when I noticed him rushing towards me. The site of him wearing a black varsity jacket and fitted, grey jeans reminded me of that thin line between love and hate; I was suddenly unsure which side I was on.

"I'm so sorry. Please, don't leave," he said as he reached the table.

A knife could've punctured my side and it wouldn't have hurt as much as hearing those words. He likely didn't remember, but they were the last ones *I* uttered before he left three years ago. With a deep breath, I willed my face into what I thought was a neutral expression and sat down. He smiled and took a seat as well.

Almost immediately, the waitress arrived to take our drink orders. Just like old times, his dimpled smile left the young woman like a ball of play-do in his hands. Naturally, she assumed he was flirting and turned her full attention to him. I understood. I knew all too well how distracting his charm, his lips could be. Even now, a part of me fantasized of leaning across the table and licking them. I shook my head to clear the image from my mind and folded my arms across my chest.

"Damn, you look like I'm about to shoot you," he said when she left.

"You know, that *would* make me feel better."

"I see you aren't going to go easy on me."

"Should I?"

"No, of course not." He sat up straighter. "Listen, this may not mean anything to you, but I am truly sorry for what happened between us."

He seemed sincere, but any man worth a nickel would know to apologize so I wasn't impressed.

"You're right, it doesn't mean a thing, but what did happen between us, Dean?"

Hushed murmurs and scraped plates filled the silence between us. The waitress arrived with the wine he ordered, and she couldn't pour it fast enough. There was no way I'd make it through this meeting without some extra assistance.

"All I know for sure is that I just wasn't ready," he said.

"Perhaps, but *I'm* sure you knew that long before you decided to tell me—a week before leaving for Buenos Aires."

"You're right," he sipped the merlot. "I just didn't know how to tell you.

I'd waited for this moment for three years. The things I needed to say. Questions I wanted to ask, yet now that I had the opportunity, I didn't want to know the answers. Seeing him was a mistake.

"So, what's up with you and Vince Parker?" He asked, catching me off guard.

"Is that the real reason you asked me here?"

"No, but I gotta admit, I'm curious."

"You mean jealous?" I said, taking a deep drink.

"A little, yes."

I paused to study his face. The tense jaw. A flicker of hardness behind light brown eyes. Was he serious? I couldn't tell, but worse than that I wished I could. Yes, seeing him was definitely a mistake. I pushed the glass away, pulled some cash from my purse and dropped it on the table.

"Goodnight, Dean."

He called out for me as I headed for the door, but I quickened my steps and pushed through the exit. I thought I'd escaped when a hand caught my elbow.

"Hey, wait. Don't leave like this."

"Sorry, but I have other plans."

Easing out of his grip, I tried to hurry to the Subway platform on the next block, but he was right at my back.

"Ok, well, can I see you again? I have an art show in a few weeks. I want you to come."

"Yeah, I doubt that will happen."

"Oh, come on, Sosh. I wanna see you before I go back to Argentina."

"Nothing has changed with you!" I whirled around. "You're still the same, selfish—"

He pulled me into his arms, leaving the rest of my words to find their way through the tangle of dreadlocks.

"I'm sorry. I'm so sorry I hurt you."

I couldn't breathe. Or rather, I refused to. Doing so would re-install his scent into my brain and leave me trying to convince it to stop playing reruns of "Sasha and Dean: The Movie". Still, I couldn't hold my breath forever. He lifted my face up then pressed our foreheads together. Lips brushed against my nose. With his teeth, he gently tugged my bottom lip then kissed me deliberate and hard. It wasn't until he pulled away—leaving me drunk and disoriented—that I finally took a breath.

"I've missed you," he said, leaving a hand on the side of my face.

And that was it. Just three words made all the feelings bubble on my skin like witch's brew in a cauldron. Just three little words dispatched the good memories on a mission to seek and destroy the bad ones. By the time good sense kicked in, prompting me to disengage our bodies and step back, the flashbacks were ready with all the moments, all the reasons I should stay in his arms.

I closed my eyes, hoping to will them away, yet it only made the visions clearer.

Chapter 9

I walked the streets of NYC in a daze, until the sound of waves brought me back to earth. I focused then and found I'd wandered onto the grassy knoll of Chelsea Piers. My shoes were in my hand; when I'd taken them off, I didn't know. All I knew was Dean's lips. I could still feel them against mine. In a moment of silliness, I'd tried wiping the kiss off. I even reapplied lip balm hoping the flavor would mask his. I was wrong. About the wiping, about the lip balm, about meeting him.

I'd made a huge mistake.

My phone buzzed for the millionth time and I finally checked it. Ten missed calls and a number of texts from Amara and Nina, asking where I was.

"Damn."

The birthday party. I'd had every intention of going, but that kiss, like some stealth virus, had wiped my memory and inserted its own set of commands.

I called Nina.

"I can't make it, something came up."

"Bullshit! You get your ass over here before I come find you," she said through her teeth before hanging up. I thought I'd done the smart thing by calling the peaceful one.

15 minutes later, I stood outside my front door, still trying to block out the images of the kiss. With no time left to stall, I put on my best smile, and went inside.

"Surprise!"

I stumbled back into the hallway. My father and younger brother, Milo, followed me out and burst into a round of "Happy Birthday". They were completely out of tune, but I didn't care. Karen, my Step-mother, ushered me inside just as Nina, Amara, and London appeared with a cake.

"What are you guys doing here and why does that thing look like a small forest fire?" I asked, hugging her neck.

"You kept saying how much you missed us, so I told dad, let's go see our girl," I hugged her again. A teeny part of me wished my real mother had come, but I knew that would never happen. For one thing, I hadn't spoken to her in years, despite the fact that she

71

lived within a 20-mile radius. Second, even if we *were* on speaking terms, she wouldn't be caught dead on this side of town unless it was for the sake of publicity. I gave Karen an extra squeeze then did the same to my dad and brother.

"What's up, man? I can't believe they were able to get you from under that pile of books you live in," I teased, pulling my only sibling in for a hug. It was a rare occasion that drew him from the confines of the library at Brown University; his 3.8 GPA was a testament to the fact.

"I thought of putting up a fight, but no one can beat Karen."

"Wow, it only took 19 years for you to figure that out." I turned to the intimate group of friends and family. "Thank you all so much. I'm so sorry I'm late."

What should have been a dining area was filled with fabrics, test patterns, and dress forms, so Nina had no choice but to set the cake on the kitchen island. My cheeks warmed as everyone gathered around. Being the center of attention wasn't high on my list of aspirations.

"OK, make a wish," Amara said.

"I'm too old for that," I laughed, "plus, I don't know what to wish for."

"A boyfriend," my brother coughed out.

"Ooh, good one," Amara said before taking off in the direction of my bedroom.

"Ooh, shut up!"

I smirked and turned my attention to the sky-blue sugary confection modeled after a Hermes Birkin bag. With one blow, I diffused all 30 candles and was awarded with a furious round of applause.

"So, what was your wish?" Nina asked.

"That you'd give me a real Birkin instead of an edible knock-off."

"Hmm, 15k for a bag, I don't love you that much."

"Surprise!" Amara yelled, just as I cut into it. I looked up to see Vince holding a bouquet of flowers and smiling shyly at her side.

Wish granted.

"Honey, if I were twenty years younger—"
I heard Karen say, but didn't tune in to the rest of the sentence. Vince was the only thing in my sights as Amara led him to the table. I didn't like the arm she'd hooked into his, but I smiled anyway. In the seconds it took for him to reach me, my mind drew up a comparison between him and Dean then quickly declared the

taller, leaner muscled Vince the winner.

"Happy Birthday." He placed the flowers in my hand then brushed his lips across my cheek, setting off a cool, blue-flamed fire in my chest.

"I would have bought a *real* gift if I'd known it was your birthday sooner."

"Dang, your stalker dossier failed again? Guess Google doesn't know everything, huh!"

"Shush," he said, poking me in the ribs. I giggled like the Pillsbury dough boy which only encouraged him to do it again.

"Ahem."

We both jumped and turned to see Karen and my father. The latter wore his "serious" face which made me laugh more.

"Alrighty, I guess introductions are in order," I clapped my hands. "Vince, this is my Dad, Lincoln, and my step-mom, Karen. Guys, this is Vince Parker."

Vince offered his brightest smile and his hand. Dad kept his stone face but returned the shake without incident.

"It's so nice to—"

"So, what are your intentions with my daughter, young man?"

"Oh, Lord," I wanted no parts of that conversation and tried my best to slide out of sight. Of course, Karen couldn't let me go so easily. She hooked my arm and slid out with me.

"So, tell me hun'. What's going on with you two?"

"Huh-uh, nothing. We're just, you know, friends."

"Hmpf," she pursed her lips. "He didn't kiss you like he's your friend, and he's certainly not looking at you like he's your friend."

I turned and caught him undressing me in the same manner I'd done not five minutes before. If he kept it up, some actual undressing was going to take place.

"We umm, well, I don't know, ok? I like him, really like him, but he can't be serious, can he?"

"He's here, ain't he?"

"Yeah, but that could just be because—"

"Look, I know you've had a rough go of things romantically, and you haven't exactly had the best examples of great relationships, but you can't let that keep you from opening up to other people. He might turn out to be a first-class jerk—"

"Exactly!"

"*Or* he could be the best thing that's ever happened to you. You'll never know unless you try."

In my heart, I knew the truth in Karen's words. Translating that to my brain was like speaking Mandarin to a French speaker and expecting a response. Involving myself with Vince meant being open to the possibility of pain; a risk my mind wasn't sure it could take.

By now, Milo had joined Vince and my father. The three of them stood in the center of the living room, laughing and joking like old friends. When Vince caught sight of me, he excused himself.

"Hello again, Mrs. Ellis. Can I borrow her for a few minutes?"

"Mmhmm," she said, elbowing me in the side before she headed back to my father.

Vince grabbed my hand and led me into the kitchen.

"Your place is really nice, though I wish you would've invited me here first."

"Speaking of invitations, who *did* invite you?"

"Hmm, she told me not to tell."

"Ah, that would be Nina."

Amara wouldn't have cared.

"So, why did you say yes?" I asked.

"Huh? What do you mean?"

"I mean, why are you here? Are you really that interested in me?"

"OK, wow. Where is this coming from?"

"I don't know…it's just—nothing."

He stepped closer to me and lowered his voice. "Does this have anything to do with that guy?"

It had everything to do with "that guy", but why did he have to be so damn perceptive?

"No," I lied. "It's to do with the fact that you're hanging out with my family and friends." I gestured to the crowd. "I mean, you've met my parents and we're not even close to dating."

"Wait, what? Not even close? Damn, I must be slipping."

"Hey, don't hog her all night!" Nina came and pulled me to the living room. We spent the next few hours singing karaoke and playing games. I even dusted off the Wii. It hadn't been used in over five years, but I was a natural at "virtual" tennis, so I maintained my undefeated record. Hours later when there was no one left to beat, and the cake was nearly done, I thanked my guest for sharing their evening with me. Amara, Nina, and Vince hung around to help clean up, but as usual, Amara did more talking than cleaning.

"So, Vince, you about ready to give up?" She asked, plopping onto the couch.

"What do you mean?"

"You know, the game? Chase her until she finally gives in then bang! Out like a light."

"Ok, it's time for us to go. Happy Birthday, Sosh," Nina slapped her shoulder then pulled her off the couch.

"What?" Amara giggled and stumbled her way to the door. "I can't be the only one who's thought of this, right Sasha."

"Good night, Amara."

I tried to slam her foot in the door as I let them out but missed by an inch. Behind me, Vince sat at a barstool gauging my reaction.

"So, umm, would you like something to drink? Coffee? Wine?" I asked, hurrying to the liquor cabinet.

"Got any whiskey?"

"Let me see."

In the cupboard, I pushed some bottles around and checked the labels. I chuckled when I found the right one and placed it on the table.

"Rough Rider?" he laughed.

"Amara's idea of a joke, I'm sure."

"Guess joking is her thing, huh?"

I responded with a shrug and passed him a glass then brewed some tea in the Keurig for myself. There was still a bit of cake left so I grabbed it and brought it to the table as well.

"You ok?"

I glanced up, stopped short when I finally realized what the hustle and bustle of the night had kept me from truly processing: Vince Parker was in my apartment. My kitchen. There could only be one explanation for such an impossibility: I'd fallen into an alternate universe. That, or he'd clearly mistaken me for someone else. Yes, that was it. I probably reminded him of some love he couldn't get over. It was the only thing that made sense.

"Sasha," he said, lifting the corner of his mouth. I prayed he wouldn't realize I was a fake.

"Yes. I'm fine, I just. I'm not sure I—"

"You believe her," he said, staring down at his drink.

"Huh?"

"Your friend, what she said. You believe I'm just in it for the chase."

"I don't, I just—ok, I don't know."

I sank against the counter and sipped the bitter tea. The truth was, Amara had spoken what I'd been feeling since day one. I'd tried to shake the feeling a dozen times, but I kept getting sucked back into a downward spiral of doubt.

"We have a problem then." He stood, walked around the counter to stand in front of me. "Here I am doing everything I can to prove I'm serious, and you're doing everything you can to prove it's not true. Maybe I need to switch up my tactics."

Vince slid an arm up my back and placed the other over my chest. His lips reached mine and while I wanted nothing more than a full surrender to his kiss, I stepped back instead.

"I was right. It is that guy."

"No, it's—"

"Then what is it, Sasha? And don't say nothing because I know you feel this," he gestured between us. "You feel it but won't let it take."

What could I say when he was right?

How about the truth?

The truth. What was the truth? I didn't know it myself so how could I tell him? Suddenly, it was the perfect time for cake. I moved to the island and took my time, cut a slice and stuffed half of it into my mouth. When I finished, I thought of going for another piece, but grabbed Vince's glass and downed the rest of the contents instead.

"That guy the other night was the one who did the photograph of me at the gallery, Dean."

"Go on."

"He's also—we also dated seriously for five years."

Vince nodded and refilled his glass. "I understand. Relationships like that can be hard to get over."

"I'm over it," I said.

"Which is why you ran away that night?"

"It's not that. I just wasn't expecting to see him, is all."

"Right, well, running is a temporary solution." He refilled his glass.

"I know, I just—things didn't end well for us and seeing him just brought all of that back to the surface." I slid into one of the barstools and he came around to join me.

"I'm not saying he's the reason I'm hesitating—"

"So, you admit it—your hesitation?"

"Yes, I'll admit that," I sighed. "I am absolutely hesitating but try to understand. It's not like you're some average dude I met at the club. You're *you*. You have to know that's a lot to handle."

"I do," he said, staring into his glass.

"Then you get it."

"I get it, but that doesn't change how I feel."

He put the drink down and held my hand.

"Sasha, I'm going to say this for what I hope is the last time. I am serious about you. I won't promise things will be perfect because we both know nothing is. But can you at least give us a chance?

He stared at me with hope blazing in his eyes. I knew the smart thing to do, but I was tired of being smart.

"Ok," I said, though only half my voice showed up.

"You're sure?"

"No, but what the hell," I said laughing.

"Honesty, wow! I like how that looks on you," he traced my ear with his thumb, sending a ripple of pleasure that weakened my knees. I gripped the back of an empty stool to steady myself as the digit slid down my neck and over my collarbone.

"We better uh—"

"Yeah. I should go," he said. "I got some early meetings, but hopefully we can catch up sometime later."

I felt my lips turning down but caught them before they reached frown status. I'd expected him to protest at least a smidge. Especially since the "I wanna get to know you speech" usually ended with a knowing in the Biblical sense. I would've turned him down of course, but I still wanted him to ask. Instead, I followed him to the door, admiring the outline of his muscles pushing through the sweater. Yes, I definitely wanted him to ask.

At the door he turned, grabbed my hand.

"I'll see you soon, right?"

"Maybe."

He inched towards me, but before his lips reached mine I slid my arms around his waist and let my head rest on his chest. The warmth radiating from him was damn near as good as a kiss. He returned the embrace and placed a kiss on top of my head.

"Come back soon," I said because I meant it.

"I will."

We stayed in each other's arms a little longer then said our goodbyes. When the door had closed, when his scent no longer surrounded me like an electric blanket, I took a deep breath and prayed I hadn't made a huge mistake.

"Hey, you're the girl dating Vince Parker, right?" A random girl on the street asked

"Nope."

I lied with a smile and kept walking before further inquiries could be made. A few weeks had gone by since we'd first made a few meager headlines, but everyone seemed to remember. That was the third person who'd stopped me, and it was starting to get on my nerves.

As a designer, I enjoyed a significant amount of notoriety in the fashion world, but I'd yet to break into the general public; it was mainly the die-hard fashionistas who knew me. This meant I was still able to walk down the street without being hassled; a commodity more valuable now that I ran the risk of losing it.

Turning off Prince St. and onto Broadway sent the point home. Strung up on a news cart were a dozen magazines, several of which my face was scattered across. I walked by without bothering to read the captions and waited near the curb.

"Nice pics!"

"Yeah, yeah." I greeted Amara with a quick hug. "I can't get used to this."

"You can try, but with get-ups like that, it will likely be in vain."

I looked down at my outfit: a simple blue—albeit short—jersey-knit dress and black knee boots.

"There's nothing wrong with my dress."

"Except it's not a dress, it's a shirt."

"It is *not* that short!" I said, though I tugged the hem down a bit.

"I can almost see your butt cheeks."

"That's because you're looking for butt cheeks and anyways, you're one to talk." I motioned to her breast-bearing ensemble.

"Hey, I'm not the one the idiot Paps are after and since we're on the subject, if you're going to be gracing the cover of such *illustrious* magazines, don't you think you should be wearing your own line?"

"Oh, just shut up and come on."

For once, she listened and followed along. Pedestrian traffic was light for a Saturday afternoon, but I wasn't complaining. My heart did a little dance when I saw the sign for Zara clothing store. I stepped inside, ready to spend a bundle when my phone chirped. It was a picture message from Nina. I opened it and damn near dropped the phone:

Nina: Have you seen this????? Is this what you were doing last night???!!!!!

"What's wrong?" Amara asked.

I could only shake my head. There were several pics of Dean and me talking...and kissing. Though it was dark, my face could be seen clearly. Dean's on the other hand, was obstructed by his dreadlocks. How had I been so stupid? They'd been following me around for weeks.

"Crap!"

"*What is wrong?*" Amara moved in front of me and shook my shoulders.

"I gotta go—double crap, I'm so dead!"

I extracted myself from her grip and headed for the nearest train, all the while concentrating on the phone. It wasn't until I reached the platform that I realized I had no clue where to go. I didn't know where Vince lived, nor did I have access to someone who could tell me; the price for not stalking him on social media like a reasonable person.

I pushed through the crowd and raced up the stairs into fresher air. After several attempts to reach him again, I decided to try the only place I knew.

The taxi had barely stopped before I hopped out and raced into the facility. I slipped past the reception desk and went to the room he'd used before but found it empty. It occurred to me to knock on some of the other doors, but I didn't want to ruin anyone's session. Instead, I sulked back to the lobby and headed for the door just as a familiar face breezed through.

"Excuse me, you're Vince's manager, right?"

After a quick glance he seemed to write me off then quickly turned back. "Oh wait, you're the girl from the papers— Sasha something or other."

"Yes!" I answered without rolling my eyes.

His smile broadened, and he threw an arm over my shoulder. "Man, the press loves you guys together. I didn't think it would work at first—they're so fickle, you know— but they're eating it up."

"I'm sorry, didn't think what would work?" I shrugged his arm off.

"Vince and a girlfriend. I told him to find someone who'd go along—publicity for the album and such. He was so adamant about not doing it— guess he changed his mind, huh."

"I don't know what you're talking about."

"Of course, you—" he stepped back and really looked at me. Saw the fire building in my bones. "You had no idea. Well, uh, he's in studio C."

I stepped around him but stopped when he caught me by the elbow.

"Hey, do you think you guys could maybe fight out here?"

"Bastard!" I said, snatching my arm from his grip.

In the elevator my heels ticked across the metal floor like a detonator. If my pulse raced any faster, I'd pass out or have a heart attack. So that was his game…parade me around like some show pony? Like some dog at a Westminster Show?

I should have known. I did know, and I'd talked myself down. No, he talked me down. Coaxed me into his arms and convinced me to take a chance. *Bastard!*

The elevator rang out like the bell at a prize fight. I stalked past the rooms and snatched the door to Studio C open without a care for what was happening inside. A wall of sound enveloped me as a rounded a corner and entered the space.

I stopped short. It wasn't a large room like the last one, but a smaller version made full by the man hunched over one of those boards with the buttons. Headphones swallowed his ears, which explained why he'd yet to turn around. I needed a plan. One that didn't include staring at the muscles in his back or watching his fingers adjust various knobs. Yet that's exactly what I did. I stood there like an idiot transfixed by his movements and the effect they had on the music flowing through the room. It was the same song he'd worked on before, except now it was ten times better.

His mellow voice blended perfectly with the instruments surrounding it. Almost enough to make me forget why I was there. I waited a moment then cleared my throat. It took a few attempts, but I was determined not to touch him.

Finally, he removed his headphones, turned around smirked.

"Come to run interference?" he flipped two knobs and the music started again, this time at a lower volume.

"I could say the—"

"Women are funny," he ignored me. "Acting all innocent like they're the ones afraid of getting hurt. Is that why you were so hesitant? Because you knew you had this dude in your back pocket?"

"It's not even like that. He's just—"

"Not like that? You fucking kissing that dude in the streets and then—fuck," he stood up and shook his head. "That's why you didn't let me kiss you, isn't it?"

"Don't curse at me," was all I could say.

He stared at me then shrugged.

"You're right. That's disrespectful and I'd hate to stoop to your level." He tried to walk around me, but I caught his arm. The muscles flexed beneath my fingers, urging me to caress them.

I released him.

"What about you?" I asked. "Your manager told me about your "faux girlfriend" plan."

"Yeah? I bet he also told you that I refused."

"You expect me to believe that? To believe this was some big coincidence?"

"You can believe whatever you want, but you might want to vacate that glass house before you start throwing stones."

This time when he walked away, I let him. He stalked to the recording booth I hadn't noticed. After fiddling with a tablet attached to the microphone stand, the music in the room changed to a bass-heavy instrumental and he began to sing.

Was it possible for a heart to have goose bumps? I felt them there, on my arms, my neck. His sultry song like a kiss on my collarbone. *Leave!* My brain screamed, but my feet walked closer to the door of glass separating us.

"*Even if the walls come tumbling down, I'm good if I got you…*" he sang, and I had to wonder if he was talking to me. *Get real! That song was probably written months ago!* True, but as he stood there singing like his life was on the line, I knew he was talking to me. *You're delusional.* Maybe.

He stopped, placed the headphones over the mic and stepped out. In the dim light, I sought his gaze and found a quiet fire blazing behind it.

"Wait," I said, grabbing his elbow before he could go back to the boards and shut me out. "I came here to say I'm sorry. The kiss—I don't know how it happened, I just—"

"Oh really? You don't know how it happened?"

"No, I just—I didn't see it coming. I didn't have a—"

"*Now* you didn't see it coming," he said, stepping closer.

"I uh, I don't—"

"So how close *was* he?"

"Huh? I don't understand the question," I said, stepping back.

"Well, I mean, he'd have to be pretty close for that to happen, right? For you *not* to see it coming?"

"I guess—no, I don't know."

Vince nodded and stepped forward, clearing the space between us.

I stepped back.

The dance continued until a wall stopped me. Stupid wall.

Vince placed his hand on either side of my face and leaned close enough for me to smell the warm, woodsy scent rising from his neck. I concentrated on the muscles of his chest, outlined by a thin sweater: the only thing separating me from his beautiful skin.

"Sasha," he said, in a tone that made my skin tingle. "Was he this close?"

I craned my neck to meet his eyes, but his mouth clouded my vision. My body hummed in anticipation as his face inched closer to mine. I closed my eyes.

"Did you see *this* coming?"

"What?" I breathed.

"You did, right? Which means you had time to move—then and now."

"What?"

I opened my eyes to find he'd taken a step back. I wanted to be angry but couldn't get my heart—or breathing—to settle from the almost kiss.

"You chose to stand there, now I'm choosing to leave."

My mind took a moment to process the words then quickly forced me into action. I lunged forward and grabbed his hand. Before I could speak, he snatched me into his arms. Into his kiss. Hands explored the curve of my waist, the swell of my thighs as they guided me back against the wall. Lovely wall.

My body, my brain, my everything melted in his arms as he pressed himself against me. I squeezed his neck, pulled my lips away then went back in for more. His kiss was more than a feeling. It was a key that unlocked every door I; a ball that wrecked every wall. I pulled away again, put some distance between us. Crossed my arms over my chest in an attempt to keep my heart from jumping out of my body.

"Fuck!" he said, swallowing the space I'd created in two long strides. "This ain't how it was supposed to happen."

He ran his thumb over my bottom lip. I waited for my brain to

82

respond, but all I managed was a blink and shake of the head.

"Open your eyes," he commanded. I obliged.

"You *will* tell me what that dude is to you."

"I told—"

He put a finger over my mouth then replaced it with his own.

"We'll settle this, but not now. Not here." He backed up; leaving my body bereft of the warmth we'd created. *What the hell?*

Chapter 10

"So, all that and he still hasn't called yet?" Amara asked, pouring another glass of champagne for herself. I'd been too busy to participate in our usual Friday night routine, but I decided to put everything on hold and concentrate on something that didn't involve a needle and thread. Happy Hour was the best compromise.

We'd chosen one of the more private lounges on her father's payroll. One that rarely hosted celebrities.

"No, he hasn't called yet," I answered.

"Yet? So, you think he will?"

I shrugged and tossed back the remaining drops of Stella Artois in my glass. I wanted something a bit stronger, but after the last night out they'd barred me from anything with more than 10% alcohol. Still, it at least took the edge off the pain.

A week had passed since the "studio rendezvous" and I'd only heard from Vince once, via text message. Granted, he was on location in Belize for a video shoot, but I was certain Verizon had a tower there.

"What I'd like to know is why did you take the manager's word over his?" Nina asked.

"We've been through this," I said, flagging the waitress down to order another round. "I don't see why his manager would lie."

"Ok, maybe he didn't lie. Maybe they did have some plan, but can't you consider it a coincidence that Vince met you during that time? I mean, the manager also said Vince refused the plan, correct?"

"Yeah right."

"You are too funny. How can you believe half of the statement, but not the other half?"

"Whose side are you on?" I asked.

"The side that makes sense. You're over here tryna drown yourself in some imported beer over a guy that *might* have used you. Meanwhile, you're still entertaining the guy that *did* use you," Nina said.

"Lord, I still can't believe she kissed that idiot."

"Can we not discuss Dean, please and thank you."

"No, we can't *not* discuss him. Wasn't that why you went to see Vince in the first place? To apologize. Did you even apologize?"

Good question. I'd been too wrapped up—literally and figuratively—to utter the words sincerely. Maybe that's what he was waiting for.

By the time I made it home, there was still too much time left in the evening and not enough alcohol in my system. I settled for a shower and as the warm water washed away the grime of the day, I thought of Vince. Maybe it was the liquor, nagging friends or the combination, but I suddenly felt like the guilty party. Hell, I *was* the guilty party. I owed him a serious apology.

With only the towel wrapped around my waist, I retrieved my phone with the intention of calling him, but saw I'd missed a message:

MrParker: Lincoln Center; 7:30

7:30! He must've been too caught up moping to hear the notification. With only 45 minutes to prepare, I raced to find an outfit that would make those pictures with Dean a distant memory.

"I guess it's safe to say you enjoyed the performance," Vince said.

"Mhmm." I nodded, unable to say anything else. He must have understood because the rest of the ride to his house was filled with only the sound of Tweet's, *My Place.*

The American Ballet Theatre's rendition of Swan Lake left me in tears. Not simply because of its beauty, but because I was reminded of what could have been. Not long ago, my dream had been to become the next African-American, principal femaledancer of their company. Biology ended that dream and now Misty Copeland was filling my Pointe shoes.

"We're here."

The sound of Vince' voice jerked me back to reality. We were parked near one of many pre-war buildings lining the street. As I waited for him to open my door, the nerves I'd successfully hidden revived themselves. Despite the beauty of the evening, a cloud had hovered quietly over the proceedings.

The doorman escorted us to the elevator and used a special key before pressing the PH button. When we reached the top, the doors opened directly into his foyer and I understood the need for special entry.

"After you," he said.

I nodded and followed his extended arm into the dimly lit foyer.

"Oh, coat and shoes here, if you don't mind."

I turned to see he'd pushed opened a panel of the wall to reveal a closet. I slipped out of both items and made a note to get one of those for my place. When he'd placed them inside, he grabbed my hand and led me through the condo.

I don't know what I'd expected. He was a guy, so I figured there'd be some sort of "mess", be it random cups or clothing here and there, but the place was beautiful and spotless.

I smell a maid!

It was a loft with huge windows, exposed brick and a balcony that circled the entire space. At its core, it wasn't much different from the warehouse he'd filmed his video in. Perhaps that was the point.

"Can I get you something to drink? Coffee? Water? Or would you like something stronger?" he said with an eyebrow wiggle.

"I'll take some wine, please."

We continued through the living room to what could have been a kitchen from a five-star restaurant and took a seat in a Lucite bar stool. Vince pulled what looked like balls of dough from the freezer, placed them on a cookie sheet and put it in the oven. He then poured a glass of wine and sat beside me.

"You're quiet tonight. What's up?" he asked.

"Nothing, I'm just processing everything."

He laughed. "Ok, well, would you like a tour while you process?"

"Please!" I said, a little too enthusiastically.

"Alright, come with me.

I followed him back through the living room and into a hallway lined with paintings, and photos of him with family and friends. He pointed out several pictures of his parents—he was the male version of his mother—and a few pictures of his siblings: two brothers and twin sisters. They all had the same rich, mahogany skin and mega-watt smiles.

Down another hallway were pictures of famous buildings and blueprints. He must have seen the expression on my face because he stopped in front of what appeared to be the floor plan of a house.

"Surprised, right?"

"Confused is more like it," I said, taking a sip of wine.

"Before I got into acting, I studied architecture in college. I have a degree and all, but I had to choose between acting or taking

86

the internships required to be licensed."

"Guess I know what you chose," I laughed. "So, have you ever considered going back? *Can you go back*, at this point?"

"I could. I've actually considered it a few times, but I don't know how many companies would risk having me there."

"Hmm, yeah I could see that. Definitely a distraction."

We continued the tour: bedrooms, guest rooms, game rooms. I kept waiting for the room lined with awards and magazine covers, but it never came. There were a few plaques here and there, but not the "testament to his greatness" I expected. In all, I couldn't believe how "normal" the place was. It was the average bachelor pad, with the addition of costly paintings and Fendi furniture. My only criticism was the size. It took up the entire 10th floor and made my place seem like a studio apartment. Which meant it wasn't *average* after all.

"Hey, so how many—wait, what smells so good?"

"Oh yeah," he pulled my arm. "Come on."

Back in the kitchen, he made a show of removing the tray from the oven then placed a scrumptious pastry in front of me.

"What is it?"

"Just taste it."

He dug into the pastry with a fork, and when he puckered his full lips to blow over it, my mouth watered for a different reason.

"Open," he said.

I obliged. The taste of peaches and a host of spices burst onto my tongue. It was like peach cobbler, but with cream and flakier dough that melted in my mouth.

"How is it?"

"Mmm," I mumbled while chewing.

"Good," he smiled, stabbing the fork into another one. "Try this one."

"They're not all the same?"

He shook his head no and held up another bite for me to taste. This one had a different filling, strawberries with a hint of lemon and mint, but it was just as delicious. In all, I tasted six different pastries, each more delicious than the last. When I couldn't eat another bite, he refilled my wine, grabbed a beer for himself and plopped into the seat next to me.

"Did you make those?" I asked.

"Yep," he beamed. "My mom taught me."

"Oh, really?"

"Yeah. She didn't believe in the whole "gender roles" thing.

She said a man should know how to cook and clean just as much as a woman should."

"Hmm, I like her already."

"She'll like you too," he said, turning to pop the top off his bottle.

I wasn't sure how to respond, so I took another sip.

"Alright. Tell me the truth."

"About?" I tried to keep my voice from breaking. We'd finally reached "the conversation" I assumed.

"About tonight. This isn't what you expected, right?" He gestured around the room.

"Oh," I laughed. "Well, I definitely thought you'd have a Vince Parker hall-of-fame somewhere."

"Ha! I appreciate that stuff, but I don't want it everywhere. I don't want to risk getting a huge ego and thinking I did all this on my own." Vince stepped down from the chair and extended his hand.

"Come on, I want to show you something."

I didn't try to hide my confusion as I followed him back through the house. Hadn't I seen all there was to see? Across from the library, he pushed through a slightly open door, pulled me inside and turned on the lights.

"Ta da!" he sang. "The previous owner was a dancer."

Fingers touched my parted lips as I was immediately thrust back into my years at Tisch School of the Arts. It was a dance studio, except it wasn't. While one wall was mirrored with a ballet barre, the opposite wall was covered with canvas paintings depicting everything from mushrooms, to a woman twirling in water as it sprayed from a fire hydrant.

"You know what this means, right?" he placed a hand on my shoulder.

"No. What?"

"We're meant to be together."

"Is that so?" I raised an eyebrow.

"Of course. It'll be great to have a real dancer in here."

This likely meant he'd had some "dancers" here already, but I kept that to myself and continued my eye-tour of the room. To the far right of the mirrored wall was an inset lounge, complete with a kitchenette, two couches and a coffee table.

"What's up there?" I said, pointing to the balcony above the picture wall.

"My office and bedroom."

A hint of excitement flashed over his face; a flush creeped into mine. Delicious food and lustful gazes would only complicate our current situation, which I was surprised he'd yet to mention.

I walked to the mirrored wall.

"God, this brings back so many memories," I said, running my hands along the cold, wooden beam. It had taken ages to choose between a full-on pursuit of dance or designing, and when I'd finally decided, I found life had other plans.

"Where are you?"

I jumped at the touch of Vince's fingers on my shoulder.

"Oh, sorry. I was in lalaland, I guess."

"It's ok. Hey, how about a dance?"

I shook my head no.

"Aww, come on."

"I haven't danced in years. I'm rusty and I'm not sure I trust my ankles."

"But you've had on heels every time I've seen you."

"That's different," I said, though flattered that he'd noticed.

"It's not, and anyway, I don't mind the rust.

"Oh, alright," I sighed.

I'd have put up more of a fight, but I really wanted to dance. I shook out my limbs and did a few, quick foot and leg stretches.

"Don't laugh," I warned.

"Never!"

He rushed to the coffee table and grabbed a remote. When the sound of Rimsky-Korsakov's Scheherazade filled the room, a familiar chill raced over my skin.

"Ok, you're definitely a stalker!"

He shrugged. "I was curious, so I watched some of your videos online. Now, stop stalling and dance."

Years had passed, but I still remembered the sequence from my audition as if I'd performed it yesterday. The sadness of the violin. The warmth of the harp. Each note tugged at my memory, tugged at my limbs until I finally rose to the balls of my feet. Guided by a swell of strings, my body twisted and leaped with a weightlessness I hadn't expected. The music pulled at some memory I couldn't bring to the surface, but I pranced and turned my way through.

It wasn't until my third pirouette— in a series of six— that the memory of meeting Dean for the first time, burst through my mind like the breaking of a dam. I stopped mid-movement, forced a smile and joined Vince on the floor.

"That was a bit rough, but it—"

89

My words were lost as he crushed his mouth against mine. It was strange, but it felt like he'd seen the memory and was trying to burn it away. I could see the scorched edges, curling from the flames until the image was slowly replaced by a new more passionate one. I was the first to pull away, but his hands remained laced in my hair as he pressed our foreheads together.

"I have to tell you something," I said.

"I know. I've been giving you time to get your words straight," he tugged my ear. "But first, tell me why in hell you stopped dancing. That was beautiful."

"Thanks. I didn't stop by choice, though."

"What happened, then?"

"Let's just say I got a little too thick for comfort."

"I don't get it." He frowned.

"In the ballet world, girls with pre-pubescent figures are the most desired," I tried to explain. "I fit the bill until my second year at Tisch, when I had this inexcusably late growth spurt that added four inches to my hips and two cup sizes to my breasts."

"Hey, I'm not complaining," he said, scanning my body.

I smiled, but he wasn't fooled.

"Alright, now let's hear it. What do you have to tell me?"

A few minutes ago, I was ready to spill the beans. But now?

"About Dean and me—" I started.

"Go on."

"Well, he and I—"

My cell phone rang out and I rushed to answer it. I smirked at the unknown number flashing on the screen and ignored it.

"Where were we?"

"I presume you were going to fill me in on your ex."

"Oh…right." Perhaps I should've answered the call and bought myself more time. "Well, to put it frankly, we—"

The phone intruded once again and this time, I took the opportunity.

"Hello?"

Amara's frantic voice filled my ears. She talked so quickly I could barely understand or get a word in.

"Amara, calm down. What's going—oh my God. Text me the address, I'll be right there."

Chapter 11

"What's going on?" Vince asked as I hurried to retrieve my coat and shoes.

"I'm sorry, but I have to go. My friend is in trouble."

"Ok. Let me come with you then." He grabbed his coat as well. "It's late. You guys shouldn't be out alone."

"Really? That's sweet of you." I slipped on my shoes. "I don't know what I'm going to do with that girl. She's always been a bit of a hot-head, but jail? Then again, I don't—"

"Wait did you say jail?" he stopped in front of the elevator.

"Yeah, I have to go bail Amara out."

"Oh man," he rubbed the back of his neck. "I'm sorry, but I don't think I can go."

"What?"

"I want to, but—"

"Then come on."

The elevator opened, but when I stepped inside he was still standing in the parlor.

"I can't," he said, holding the doors open. "You know the paps have been crazy. If they catch me there—I can't risk it, I'm sorry."

A small yet rational voice in my brain said he was right. The press would enjoy nothing more than to report he'd been arrested for xyz without facts. The money they'd make from sales was worth having to print a retraction two months later in size eight font.

I knew all this and yet, I didn't care. I wanted him not to care.

"Fine." I pushed the "L" button.

"Sasha, don't be like this. You know I would if I could."

"It's fine, really. I'll see you later."

"Are you sure?"

"Yep."

He placed a timid kiss on my lips. I smiled inside when I didn't return the gesture. With him back in the parlor, the steel doors ground to a close. *Men!* When would they learn that *fine* never meant *fine?*

Standing outside the 19th precinct on the Upper East Side, I

91

knew two things:

1. I wasn't sure.
2. I damn sure wasn't fine.

At present, there wasn't a thing I could do about either, so I forged ahead. Inside, I'd expected it to be swarming with hard-nosed detectives and bad guys trying to escape, but it was quiet. Too quiet. I'd never set foot in a Police station for fear that by some extraordinary mistake, I wouldn't be allowed to leave. I approached the desk clerk with caution.

"Hi, I'm not really sure how this works, but I'm here for Amara Patel."

"Sure. We just need you to sign these forms and $500, cash."

"What is she being held for?"

"Looks like Disorderly Conduct."

Why am I not surprised? I always knew Amara's mouth would land her in trouble, but I never thought the trouble would come in the form of an 8x8 cell with iron bars. I thought she had the sense to stop herself before letting things get that far. I'd given her too much credit.

Though the station had failed to meet my expectation, I couldn't take another minute inside. As soon as I'd signed the papers and paid the fine, I stepped out into the night air and waited. By now, I should've been tangled in the sheets with Vince. If I was honest, it hurt that he'd decided not to come with me. The rational side of me knew protecting his career was the right thing. But the irrational side wanted him to put me first. It was silly, but...

"Sasha, oh my God, thank you so much."

I turned to see Amara rushing down the steps. Her cropped hair bounced at her shoulders. It wasn't until she reached my side that I noticed the signs: scraped forearms, bruising under the left eye and a shirt that probably cost a month of my salary, torn at the collar.

"Amara, when are you going to grow up?"

"I'm fine, Sasha. Thanks for asking."

"You're welcome." I headed to the waiting car with her on my heels.

"Aren't you going to ask what happened?"

"Do I really need to? Someone pissed you off and you got in a fight. Did I miss something?"

"Damn, you're really a bitch sometimes, you know that?"

"What do you want me to say? You're a grown ass woman still fussing and fighting in the streets like some teenage girl.

"I had a good reason! She was—"

92

"I'm sorry, but no reason is good enough for that."

In the backseat of the black sedan, she stroked the scratches on her arm and winced. I almost felt sorry for her, but it was about time someone put her in her place.

"I should've called Nina," she said as we pulled off.

"I wish you would have. I could've been snuggling up with Vince right about now."

"Oh, so that's where your loyalties are? With some guy who clearly has a dozen other chicks on the payroll? Some guy you swear you aren't interested in, and yet—"

"Yet what? Why is it a problem if I *am* interested? Weren't you the one telling me to settle down?"

"The problem isn't him, it's you."

"What's that supposed to mean?"

"It means as always, you pick the wrong guy."

"I pick—wow, ok, sir, can you pull over? I'm done here," I said.

"No, I'm done," she said, throwing the door open before the car reached the curb. A chorus of horns filled the night as she stepped out. With the door still open, she rifled through her purse then tossed a wad of cash onto the seat.

"That's for bail."

I reluctantly pulled the bills together but didn't have to count to know it was too much.

"You don't have to pay me back."

"I do if I don't want it thrown in my face at some later date."

"I wouldn't do—"

She slammed the door shut and stalked to the sidewalk, daring the cars to hit her. I looked down at the stack of hundreds in my hand. It must've been nice to have money to blow on a night in jail. Nice to spend life playing around or pretending to be an adult from time to time. I couldn't afford such frivolity.

My parents were well-off, but my father made me sign a contract when he'd funded my first collection, so I knew he wouldn't entertain paying for me to play around. Maybe I shouldn't have entertained it either by bailing her out and thus enabling her.

Whatever the case, it wasn't my life. After instructing the driver where to go, I let the soothing sounds of classical Cello work the anxiety away. I might have fallen asleep had the phone not vibrated against my thigh:

MrParker: Sasha, I'm sorry. Are you ok? Come back.

I suppressed the smile playing at the corners of my mouth. No message, no matter how sexy would make me forgive him so easily. That was the problem with men these days. They were all spoiled by the convenience of technology. All they knew was send a message here or DM there to make it alright.

No one was willing to go the extra mile anymore. No one was willing to do anything other than— *is that Vince's Audi?* I moved closer to the window as the driver pulled up to the curb in front of my building. The tints were too dark for me to see inside, but that had to be him. I instructed the driver to let me off a few car lengths behind the luxurious sedan.

What to do? I couldn't just walk up and tap on the window. If it wasn't him, it could be a rich psycho waiting to snatch the first dummy curious enough to approach. I chose the next best option and actively ignored the vehicle as I walked to my building at a turtle's pace.

When I was sure he—or whoever—could see, I stopped and pretended to search for something in my purse. The bag wasn't large, and I could only pretend for so long before looking crazy. "Oh well." I shrugged but couldn't shake the disappointment.

You could've gone to him.

"I could have," I mumbled, crossing the lobby to call the elevator. Everyone must have been asleep or out because it appeared much faster than usual. I twirled a lock of hair while counting down the numbers as they dropped.

A soft ding echoed throughout the lobby. When the doors eased apart I started to walk inside then stopped. Only an hour had passed since I'd last seen him, but my heart danced a meringue-like rhythm as Vince appeared.

Chapter 12

Jeans. Leggings. Jogging pants. The fate of the world rested on that choice. Well, not really though it certainly felt that way as I stood in front of my drawers. One choice was stiff, the other too loose. I didn't want Vince to think I didn't care, but I didn't want it to seem like I'd tried to hard either.

Ugh! Why was I over-thinking this? I swiped a pair of slim-cut jeans from the drawer, slipped a comfortable V-neck tee over my head and joined him in the kitchen.

He sat at the counter, brow furrowed in concentration as he read something in his phone. One set of fingers scrolled through while the others stroked his mustache. The site of him in my house, in my kitchen—relaxed as if it were his own. I could get used to it though I knew I shouldn't. If the previous events of the evening were any indication, a life with him meant a list of do's and don'ts. *It also means having him!*

I ignored the voice in my head and turned the music player to soft jazz. He looked up then and the smile that eased onto his lips only reminded me of how painful it would be when I landed back in the real world.

"How long have you been standing there?" he asked when I entered the kitchen.

"Not long. Can I get you anything?"

"Coffee?"

"Umm, the only thing I have is instant. I don't drink it much and that seems to be the best way to keep it fresh. It's good though."

He looked skeptical.

"Just try it."

My skin heated as he watched me assemble the necessary items. When I finished mixing and placed the steaming cup in front of him along with a tray of muffins I'd purchased, he just stared at me.

"What?"

"Nothing." He glanced down and took a tentative sip. "Not bad."

"See!"

I fixed a cup of tea for myself then slipped into the barstool next to him.

"Sasha. I said it before, but I really am sorry about tonight."

"It's ok."

"It's not, and the sad part is I wish I could say it won't happen again, but we both know that's not true. All I can say is, in the future I'll try to make the instances as few as possible."

The future? Did he see me in his future? Did I see him in mine?

"You're right," I said, trying not to get my hopes up. "Tonight was definitely disappointing, but I understand. When I stepped back from the moment, I realized the issue it might have caused."

Again, he stared at me as if I'd suddenly grown an extra eye or maybe lost one.

"What? Why do you keep staring at me?"

"I don't know. I guess I'm not really sure what to make of you."

"Which means?"

"I'm not used to this. Most of the women I've dated were demanding to say the least. That or they pretended to understand my lifestyle, but threw it in my face whenever they got the chance. Is that what's going on here?"

He turned his full gaze on me, let it wander over my face then slowly down the rest of my body. It was impossible to speak when I could hardly breathe, but I made an attempt.

"Umm, what—what was the question?"

"Nevermind," he laughed, severing the trance.

When I regained my composure, I decided to ask some questions of my own.

"This is off topic, but it seems like you get a lot of free moments for down-time. Is that a fluke? Have I been getting used to you being around for nothing?"

"You like having me around?"

"Maybe."

He laughed and returned to his coffee though it had to be a lukewarm mess, by now.

"Would you believe me if I said I purposely cleared those moments?"

"I guess, but why would you?" I asked, finishing the last bit of tea.

"Done?"

I nodded. Vince collected the dishes, took them to the sink and started washing.

"What are you doing?"

"Oh, sorry," he shrugged. "It's a habit. My mother always made us wash after we used something."

I joined him at the sink. There were only a few items, but it didn't feel right to let him do it alone.

"So, why'd you take the time off."

"Two reasons." He filled the basin with detergent and water. "One, I really needed it and two, I wanted time get to know you."

I caught the plate before it slipped out of my hand and onto the floor. God had a funny way of doing things. For three years, I couldn't keep a relationship to save my life; now two men were telling me they wanted me in some way. This was either a cruel joke or an ill-timed stroke of luck. I was willing to bet on the former.

"Speaking of time off, when's our next date?"

"Uh, next date?" I said, feeling the heat flood my cheeks.

"Yes, next date." He splashed me with suds. "Where you wanna go?"

"Hmm, I don't know. Maybe a basketball game."

Vince did a double take. "You're kidding, right?"

"No," I laughed. "I'd love to see a game at the Garden, though I must admit, I am *not* a Knicks fan."

"Oh Lord!" he put a soapy hand over his chest. "Just when I thought she was perfect."

"Sorry to *burst your bubbles*," I laughed.

"So wait, what's your team then? God help me, if you say the Bulls," he said, lifting his hands to the sky.

"Ok, can you guys get over those 54 points Jordan dropped? That was what, over 20 years ago?"

"Lord, Lord, Lord." He stumbled back and collapsed into a barstool. His eyes glazed over like a deer in headlights before he shook himself out of it.

"What?" I asked.

"Yo, we're on Candid Camera, or Punk'd, right?" he looked around. "Nah, nah. John Quinones is bout to jump out the closet or something."

"I don't think so." I smiled sweetly while rinsing the rest of the dishes.

"This ain't real. No woman is smart, sexy, and loves, I mean *loves* Basketball."

"Man, what kind of women are you meeting? You do know there's a whole ass league full of said women, right?"

"I know, I know, but they seemed like exceptions to the rule."

I shook my head, dried my hands and slid onto the seat next to him.

"So, ok, ok. You ain't feeling the Knicks, who's your team then?"

"Oh, that's easy. Any one Lebron is on."

"And the shoe drops!" he sank in his chair and rubbed hands over his head. "I knew there had to be something."

"What? What's wrong with Lebron?" I whined.

"Nothing, it's just I see now that you're not really a Basketball fan. You're a *Lebron* fan that just happens to know a bit about the game."

I shrugged; nothing could be said when he was right.

"Well, at least that's something to work with," he sighed. "Stick with me long enough and I'll make you an expert!"

"Mhmm," I mumbled, turning to fidget with the frayed edges of a fabric bolt leaning against the counter. Dean had said the same thing in reference to photography, but didn't stick around long enough to keep his word.

"What's the matter?"

"Huh?" I looked up. "Oh, nothing. I'm fine."

"You're a bad liar."

"No, really. Its—"

"It's that guy, right?" he nodded. "Man, I wanted to fuck him up when I saw that pic in the paper. Every time I feel like I'm getting somewhere with you, he shows up or does something to pull you back. Is there something I need to worry about?"

"Huh?" The conversation had turned so quickly, I had no clue what to say.

"Between the two of you. Is there still something going on?"

"About that...I tried to tell you at the house. He *was* my fiancé."

Vince turned to me with eyes hardened by understanding.

"Ok, that's who he was before. I want to know who he is to you now."

I wanted to know the same thing, but for now I said:

"No one."

"So, there's no one stopping you from seeing me."

"I do see you. I know how you—"

"Nah, you hear what I say, but you don't believe it. You don't believe that I could want you, but you will."

He placed a hand on the back of my neck and the other on my cheek, caressing it with the pad of his thumb. He drew me towards him and placed the softest of kisses on the crown of my head. He then kissed my forehead. Pulled me in closer. Kissed the tip of my nose.

"I want you to see me, and me only." He kissed my palm. "Can you do that?"

I'll do anything you say, I thought, but what I said was: "Umm, ok."

"You're serious?" He cupped my face in his hands.

Truthfully, I didn't know if I was or wasn't, but staring in his eyes, there was only one thing I could say.

"Yes."

How had we gone from washing dishes to making pledges of exclusivity? I couldn't say, but as his body inched closer, rational thought melted away until there was only his mouth on my mouth...on my neck, on my shoulders, burning through the flimsy fabric of my shirt. It wasn't until he'd inched it above my stomach that I realized what was happening.

"Vince," I stayed his hand. "This is too—too fast."

"If you want me to stop," his tongue was like silk against my neck. "Just say the word and I will."

He turned me around and sent shivers over my body as full lips brushed across my back. I did want him to stop, sort of. The problem was that the words had taken refuge in the recesses of my brain and refused to come out.

"Mmm," I moaned when his hand slipped over my breast.

"Sounds like yes to me," he cupped them. Massaged them. "Say it."

"Say what?" I breathed.

"Say yes."

He ran a thumb over my nipples. Placed soft kisses along my neck and shoulders that sent my brain into overload as it tried to process the sensations he created.

"Yes."

A gentle moaned escaped as he finally eased the shirt over my head and put every nerve on high-alert.

"Turn around."

I obliged

"Move your hands!" he said, nodding towards my covered breasts.

I did as I was told, allowing them to rest in their natural position.

"You're beautiful, you know that?"

Under normal circumstances, I would have been more than flattered, but I couldn't help wondering how many times he'd offered that flattery to others.

"What? What did I say?" Vince asked, worry clouding his gorgeous features.

"Nothing, its fine."

He reached for my arms and guided me to the couch.

"Sasha, why is it that every time I give you a compliment, you act as if it's an insult?"

"I don't know Vince, it's just..." I shrugged.

"It's just what, Sasha? Tell me the truth."

"Well, you've probably been with so many women and I don't know...I guess I sometimes feel like this has all been done before." I shook my head and sighed. Deep down, I knew the reasoning was a bit childish, but it didn't change the way I felt.

"I'm just like every other guy you've dated. Well, not in every sense, but the fact is, every man you've dated has been with some other woman at some time." Vince grasped my hands and pulled me closer.

"It doesn't make anything I say to you less truthful."

He had a point.

"You know," I began, tucking a lock of hair behind my ear, "if someone told me one day I'd have a topless therapy session with Vince Parker, I'm quite positive I would have said something along the lines of "when pigs fly".

He grinned, pulling me until I was nearly on top of him.

"You see, that's what I like about you. I never know what you're going to say."

"Kiss me," I murmured.

The words were hardly out of her mouth before his tongue replaced them. His kisses were firm, yet not overpowering and the combination left me light-headed. I leaned into his body, pushing against him until I was completely on top.

With fevered kisses, I moved from his face to his neck and back. I wanted more. Needed more of him. I yanked at the buttons on his shirt and smiled when the silky-smooth skin was within my grasp. Since the first time we'd met, I'd thought of nothing more than what I would be like to have him beneath me. I slid my hands over the muscular ridges of his torso. The moans of pleasure that seeped from his lips gave me chills.

Suddenly, he sat up, locked my legs around his waist and carried me to my bedroom. *How does he know where your room is?* Who cares!

Gently, he placed my body atop the sheets, caressing my skin as he eased the jeans off. His kisses left dots in my vision as he crawled up my body and a small voice wondered if it was all a dream.

Chapter 13

By the time Monday rolled around, the dream had morphed into an anxiety-provoking hallucination. Since then, "what have I done?" was the only question strolling through my mind on repeat. I'd scrutinized each replay, but still arrived at the same conclusion: I'd lost my mind. Seriously. Why else would I sleep with a guy who pretended to be in love with women for a living?

He talked a good game! Boy, did he talk a good game. But it wasn't just talk; he'd back it up with hands that played my body like a Baby Grand. Even now if I closed my eyes and concentrated, I could feel them caressing my thighs, my back, my—

I jumped when a notification rang out from phone.

MrParker: Hi beautiful. I'm so sorry, but can we reschedule tonight? I have a reshoot.

☹ ☹ ☹ I responded.

MrParker: I know, I know. I'll make it up to you, promise.

I tossed the phone on the desk and walked to the window. Was it already starting? The lead-up to the big brush off?

"Ugh! Stop it."

"Stop what?" London appeared behind me.

"Nothing, nothing. What's up?"

"We've got a problem. Two, actually."

"Let me guess. More pics online?"

"I wish." She sat down. "The buyer from Neiman's called and they need us to re-work the initial designs for the pop-up shop."

"What? How many styles?"

"All styles. They need the production costs to come down about 7%."

"Are you kidding me? They already approved everything. Production has already started."

"I know, and I told them. They said they're willing to pay 30% of the fees incurred."

"Oh, they're going to pay all of it. Have Nina contact their CFO and inform our attorney just in case."

I pulled up the design specs and shook my head. 15 pieces. All in need of new flat specs, new patterns, new cost work ups, new test fits, new samples. This would inevitably set the shipping date back, which meant more complaints. Of course, they'd never remember they caused the delay in the first place.

While London brought Nina up to speed, I settled what I could on my end. After setting a new deadline for samples with the design team, I met with production and held a conference call with the warehouse. When the last call was complete, it was after 6:30.

By the time I made it home, I was glad Vince had canceled our date. I couldn't see how I would've made it through dinner and a show without dozing off. Still, it was disheartening to know I'd have to wait a week to see him again. Movie shoots and promotional tours officially sucked.

After a quick shower restored my power level, I headed to the kitchen for a bedtime cup of tea. Just as I removed a mug from the cabinet, the doorbell rang.

Who in the world…Vince? My heart raced with my feet to the front door. A quick glance through the peephole made me wish I'd been quieter. I unlocked the door but left the chain on.

"What are you doing here?"

"Hello to you too, Sasha. Can I come in?"

"Can you come in? You can't just show up at my place unannounced, Dean."

"Sasha, please?"

I unchained and opened the door but heaved the biggest sigh I could muster to let him know I wasn't happy. Having him in the apartment was stranger than having Vince over. I didn't know whether to sit or stand. Finally, I sat in an arm chair—as far away as I could sit without being rude. I wasn't down long before Dean's lingering gaze on my chest reminded me of the skimpy red romper I'd put on.

"I'll be back."

I rushed to retrieve a robe from the bathroom then took my place back in the arm chair.

"OK, Dean. What is it?"

"Nothing," he smiled, "I was just in the neighborhood and wanted to stop by."

I hated what his smile did to me. A contagion that left my body weak and my heart broken.

"I haven't heard from you in three years yet suddenly you want to stop by. I know you have a show going on, but that doesn't mean you have to reconnect with me."

"Actually, it does. That's part of why I'm here. I want you to

103

come to the show. I know your birthday already passed, but it's sort of my gift to you."

"Amazing," I said with a laugh.

"What?"

"You haven't changed one bit. We both know you should be on your knees begging for forgiveness."

"Sasha, it's not—"

"No, it is. You're still a selfish son of a bitch. Do you know how hard it was for me? You asked me to marry you. *Marry you*, Dean," I stood up. "You knew how I felt about marriage, about my real mom and her parade of husbands. You knew how hard it was for me to say yes, but I did. I said it and what did—no," I threw up my hands. "You know what, I can't have this conversation right now."

I stalked into the kitchen and headed straight for the Vodka. I downed two shots and stared into the living room. *Who the hell does he think he is?* Three years he'd been gone, and he expected my forgiveness in three minutes.

I was angry, obviously. But a small part of me couldn't help rejoicing at the chance to see him again. Couldn't help feeling that having him back was what I really wanted. Still, the larger more important voice was telling him to piss off. That was until he walked towards me and made all the voices shiver. Even pissed off, I had to acknowledge the flicker of arousal.

He wasn't as tall as Vince but what he lacked in stature was easily made up for by his build. Strong with thick muscles he'd maintained since his years as a running back in college. I knew every plane, every angle of those muscles which was why I avoided his eyes when he stood against the island in front of me.

"Sasha," he reached for my hand. I pulled away.

"Sasha, I'm sorry. I realize my mistakes. There are so many I don't know how to begin to make up for them, but I can't let you go again. I don't want to lose you."

"Looks like you're a little late for that party." I tossed back the contents of my glass and turned to pour another round.

"What do you mean?"

"For one, you lost me a long time ago. For two, I'm off the market."

"So, what, you're saying you and Vince Parker are dating?"

"That's exactly what I'm saying." I smiled and downed another shot. That had to be my second or third, or was it my fourth? I knew I had to stop before I ended up doing something else I couldn't remember.

"Oh, come on, Sasha. How long have you known this guy?" He laughed.

The glass nearly shattered as I slammed it onto the granite countertop.

"You got a lot of nerve coming here questioning my—"

Dean's hot and furious lips swallowed my words. I felt like the young heroine of a vampire novel except this wasn't some hormonal teenage werewolf trying to worm his way into my heart. It was a man. A strong, sexy man who knew exactly what buttons to push to leave me like butter in his hands.

Calloused yet somehow smooth hands that caressed the sides of my neck before slowly moving down my torso and settling around my waist. He fisted my hair and elicited an urgent moan, which only made him bolder. Dean pulled me closer, delved deeper into my mouth. His hands down my back then hoisted me onto the counter, all without separating our lips.

My mind was a ball of mush, but two tiny voices returned to wage war. It was only when I felt Dean's fingers pulling my straps down that I was able to make out what they were fighting about.

"I can't...do this."

Dean continued his oral assault of my neck and collarbone while his hands massaged my thighs.

"I know you still have feelings for me," he whispered against my skin.

"Yes but," I panted, gathering up all my strength to push him away. "That's not enough."

It took a few moments, but he removed his hands from my breasts and hugged me tight before pulling me down from the counter. He kept his arms around my waist as he spoke.

"I won't let you go."

"You don't have a choice."

I stepped out of his arms, walked to the front door and opened it.

"Good night, Dean."

A moment later, he paused at my side.

"I mean it, Sasha." With the pad of his thumb, he caressed the side of my face and smiled. "I won't let you go this easily."

Chapter 14

Aroma Coffee was mostly empty when I walked inside. It was probably for the best. Amara and I had yet to really talk since her stint in the clink, and I was sure both our frustrations would bubble up at some point in the conversation. I only hoped we'd be able to smooth things out quickly and quietly. Vince was back and had plans to take me out. I'd hate to show up with a coffee-stained sweater.

Amara looked up and offered a half-smile then continued typing on her phone. Her fingers moved across the touch-screen in rapid succession. She was a shoe-in winner for a text contest should she ever take the time to enter.

"Hello," I said, sliding into the cushioned, steel chair.

She returned the greeting then tucked the phone into her purse. An awkward silence settled around us as we glanced out the window. At our hands. At the door. Anywhere except each other. It was Nina's idea that I "clear the air" with her. I'd asked for an explanation as to why, but she just kept pushing for a meeting. I should've made her come with us. At least then we would have had a referee.

"So...how have you been?"

"Fine," Amara said, watching the pedestrians rush by.

"That's good."

I joined her in people watching. They scurried through the streets like mice over subway tracks. It didn't matter what time it was or where they were going, New Yorkers were always in a hurry.

"So, are you going to apologize or what?"

"Huh?"

"That's why we're here, right? Or at least why we should be here," she said.

"What exactly am I apologizing for?" I asked.

"For being an insensitive bitch."

"What are you—?"

"Did you see these scratches? Did you see the bruise under my eye? You couldn't have missed it, yet you didn't bother to ask if I was ok, or even what happened. As usual, you went straight to judgment."

I glanced at the smooth, cooper skin of her thin arms. Scabs had formed over the marks, but they were still there along with a slight bruise beneath her eye.

"You're right," I sighed. "I'm sorry. I should've said it then, but you—"

"Like I said, judgement," she laughed, "and all for defending you."

"What—what do you mean? What happened?"

"Oh, now she wants to know!" she said to the woman at the table next to us.

"What happened, Amara?"

"Nothing really, I just punched a chick in her face because she called you a gold-digging bitch."

"Amara, I—"

"I mean really, if she's going to insult you, she could at least get the facts straight. Bitch? Yes. Gold digger? No."

"Amara, I'm so sorry, I should have—"

"Of course, you should have blah, blah, blah, but instead, you always feel like you have to tell me what to do or how to run my life. Can't you just be a friend to me?"

I stared at her…

"What have I been, if not a friend? Are friends supposed to condone your bad behavior? Supposed to watch you hurt yourself without stepping in? All I've ever done is tried to help you."

"All you've ever done is criticize my every move. Always pointing out the fact that I don't have a job or saying I mooch off my dad. Meanwhile, you have no problems when you benefit from the mooching via free Champagne or getting the permits on your store pushed through because of his connections." She leaned forward and crossed her arms on the table. "If I didn't know any better, I'd think you were jealous."

"Jealous of what?"

"Jealous of the fact that my father gives me whatever I want, while yours makes you and your brother jump through hoops like circus dogs."

When had our friendship reached this point? Both of us making assumptions and accusations about the other. Had I been so caught up in my own issues that I'd failed to see the problems, stretched like too-tight seams, in my friendships?

"I can admit that sometimes I wish my dad wasn't such a hard-ass, but contrary to what you think, I'm glad he made us earn things instead of just giving it to us. It taught me to work for what I want and how to value it when I get it."

"So now you're saying I don't value what I have?"

"Do you? Other people work their asses off to get opportunities you throw away like bread crusts."

"Ok, I'm done," she stood up and collected her purse.

"Amara, don't leave. We're adults and under all this drama we're friends. Let's just settle this here and now."

She thought for a moment then plopped back onto her seat.

"I'm sorry if I made you feel like you were being judged. That was never my intention. You're my friend and I love you and I want to see you happy. That's the bottom line. If you feel like you're happy doing what you're doing, then I promise I won't say another word about anything. Now tell me," I said, reaching across the table to grab her hands. "Are you happy?"

"Define happy…"

We both smiled. Genuine smiles shared between friends who knew each other's faults and still chose to stick together. The cheerful expression slipped away before I could stop it.

"What's wrong?" She asked.

"I kissed Dean."

"Girl," she pulled her hands back. "What the hell is wrong with you?"

I relayed the story of Dean showing up at my house but left out the juicy parts in which he copped several feels. They'd win no points with this crowd.

"Why did you even let him in?"

"I don't know…I guess I just wanted to hear what he had to say."

"I guess you found out." Amara laughed.

"So, what did Vince have to say about all this?"

I ignored the question and grabbed the menu from its holder.

"Well…" she pressed.

"Well, I kind of haven't told him yet."

"OK, I'm confused. Didn't you say he came back from his trip a few days early?"

"Yeah, but I was so happy to see him, I didn't want to ruin it."

"Oh, my Lord, you sound like those idiot girls from Rom-Com movies," she rolled her eyes. "You know, they hide the secret that's not a big deal until it blows up in their face, three quarters into the movie!"

"It's *not* a big deal, Amara."

But I wasn't really sure. The kiss from Dean made me realize that I still had feelings for him though the fact that I was able to prevent the situation from going any further said a lot.

This meant the best thing to do would be to confess because if the kiss really meant nothing, it shouldn't be a problem to tell. Plus, I wanted our relationship to be as honest as possible. When I thought about it, I knew the right thing to do, but wasn't sure if I wanted to risk it.

"On second thought, don't tell him. No need to cause tension for nothing."

"That was a quick change of heart," I pointed out. "What happened to all that stuff about the Rom-Com blow-ups?"

"Man, that's just the movies. Things have to blow-up in order to push the storyline. That kind of stuff doesn't happen in—hold on."

She fished the vibrating phone out of her purse and scrolled through the screen. At my side, I felt mine do the same, but I let it go unanswered.

"Girl, my twitter feed is blowing up! Looks like—why is it about you?"

"Me?" I leaned forward.

"Yeah, hold up." She clicked through a few screens and...

"Umm, you might want to see this."

"What?" I asked, grabbing the phone from her extended hand. I glanced at a photo then handed it back. "It's fine. I'm used to it now. They could have at least published a better photo of me."

"Umm, are you wearing your contacts?"

"No, but I have my glasses, why?"

"You might want to put them on."

I shrugged, retrieved my glasses out of my bag and took another peek. My stomach churned. It wasn't a bad pictured of me, but rather a decent picture of another woman with Vince.

The walls were up, and not just the ones in my forthcoming retail store. As I pushed through the newly installed glass doors, my usual sense of pride was dampened by the latest issue with Vince. If Twitter was to be believed, I'd been replaced faster than an iPhone. Sure, a few die-hard fans came to my defense, but the majority had deemed me old news. Fine. I could be an asshole, too. The only date he'd have was with my voicemail.

"Hi, Sasha. How's it going?" the site manager looked up from his drafting table.

"It's going. Can't ask for much more." *Except maybe a man that can be faithful.*

"Very true," he said, smiling. "I have a surprise for you."

I followed him through a curtain of plastic and squealed with delight. They'd finally installed the floating staircase. For me, this was the focal point of the store, and after several heated discussions, we'd finally agreed on a design that was both beautiful and safe. Having it installed ahead of schedule gave me one less thing to worry about.

I thanked him profusely and stepped back to admire the picture that not too long ago had only existed in my head. It was still unbelievable to see so many of my life-goals coming to fruition. Yet like all good news, the bad wasn't far behind.

When everyone left for the day, I pulled up the photo again on my tablet. It was torture looking at some strange woman smiling up at him, but I couldn't help it. I'd known something like this would happen eventually, but it still hurt to see. With a sigh, I placed the tablet on the workman's table.

"Here you are."

I glanced up to see Vince standing in the doorway then turned my focus to a set of blueprints. *Nina, Nina.* Why in the world was she giving him so much access to my life? He'd already called a dozen times. Guess he didn't get the hint.

"What's going on? I've been trying to reach you for the last hour. I went to the office and you weren't there so Nina sent me here?"

"I'm busy," I said, trying not to smile at the idea that Vince Parker was looking for me.

"Busy? We had plans tonight."

"I forgot."

I picked up another set of blueprints. I could care less about them, but I needed something to focus my attention on.

"Sasha, stop acting like you can read these and tell me what's going on?" he snatched the prints from my hands then turned me to face him. His touch was like a jolt of lightning, shocking me into staring up at him.

"This isn't going to work out."

"What's wrong? What happened?"

Did he really expect me to believe he didn't know? I picked up the tablet and shoved it towards him. "This happened."

"Don't tell me you believe this crap."

"Honestly, I don't know what to believe."

"Believe *me*," he said, tossing the tablet onto the table. "How is it you can latch on to words of people you've never met, but can't do the same for me?"

"Because I can't trust you!"

"And you trust some losers sitting up in an office, trying to figure out how to ruin my life? Or maybe you trust those social media gossips who'd want nothing more than to see me drop you."

"Isn't that your plan?" I yelled.

"What the—" he came towards me with an intensity that forced me to retreat.

"I know I said this before, but must I stamp it on you as well?"

"What are you—?"

Before I could stop him, he'd pulled me into his chest and attacked my mouth. It was the only way to describe the sensation of his lips crashing against mine. If I thought we'd kissed before, I must have been asleep. This kiss was unlike any of the others from him and anyone else. But I was tired of men interrupting me, using their strength and charms to keep me from getting answers.

I brought my hands to his chest and pushed, which only made him work harder to break my resolve. He unwound his hands from my hair, slid them over my hips and brought them to rest against my behind.

"You're not playing fair," I mumbled.

"Who's playing?"

He squeezed our bodies together. Shortened breaths that were already hard to come by. *OK, two can play that game!*

I pushed again, this time with all the force I could muster. He staggered back into the work bench, finally releasing my mouth. Even as my lungs greedily sucked in air, I wanted him back. Wanted his lips back, his hands back.

"This is why I don't trust you," I said between breaths. "My body can't decide whether to kiss you or punch you."

"Why would you punch me?" he asked, removing his sweater. "What have I done to—?"

It was my turn to interrupt. I rushed him. Threw my arms around his neck, legs around his waist. Biting. Nibbling. Kissing. I assaulted him with all as if it were the last time. The kisses grew deeper, harder.

My fingers fumbled with the button on his jeans then shoved them down. The cable-knit dress I wore slipped easily over my head. He picked me up again and placed me on the first surface he

111

could find. I hummed as strong hands slid up my body, kneading the flesh along the way.

Fingers slipped beneath thin straps—slipped beneath delicate lace and hovered. His hungry gaze raked the length of my body before coming to rest on my face. Breath caught in my throat as his impassioned glare sought to burn me, to brand me, to stamp me. Lips and fingers inched closer and as they connected with my body I knew I was his.

Chapter 15

The sun squeezed through the leaves and dotted the bubbling brick fountain with a kaleidoscope of light. Fresh flowers perfumed the air and added to the serenity of the bustling garden. The stillness of the area made me forget about the busy city streets just outside the revolving doors.

I'd stumbled upon the garden—tucked in the atrium of a landmark building— via an Architectural Digest magazine. Since then I'd found it to be a great place to sketch or simply take a time-out from the everyday hustle of Manhattan life…and nosy best friends.

"I still can't believe it," Nina said.

"Can't believe what?" I asked, though I already knew the answer.

"You and Vince. I can't believe you guys had sex in your store—on a stack of drywall."

"Believe it."

I turned my attention back to the drawing, a sheath dress with a pattern similar to the brick work on the fountain. Nina shook her head and bit into a double cheeseburger. She was the only person I knew who could eat whatever, whenever without gaining weight. On top of that, the only time she worked out was when I forced her to go. How she kept the pounds off was a mystery the world would love to solve.

"I didn't know you were such a freak."

"Don't talk with your mouth full."

She nodded, finished the bite and said: "And, I can't believe you did it in public! What if someone peeped through the door or recorded you guys?"

I stared at the shrub in the center of the fountain. Why hadn't I thought about that? *Because you can't think of anything when his hands are on you!* That was certainly true, but some sort of whistle should've gone off in my head. I glanced around the jungle-like grounds, the glass-encased offices shining like stars, just beyond the perimeter. Was someone watching now? I shuddered at the thought then shook it away. With the problems on my list, I couldn't afford to add paranoia. Still, I made a mental note to be more careful.

"Is that the only reason you tracked me here?" I asked.

"No," she paused, pulling the leaf off a nearby shrub. "Ardene Group had to pull out."

"What?"

"It's nothing to do with the press we've been getting. They have a lawsuit going on and their assets are frozen until the case is over."

"What the hell did they do?"

"I don't know, but don't worry. I'll handle everything. Just focus on getting the next batch of samples."

"But how are we—"

"I said, don't worry." She nudged my side. "I'll handle it."

I nodded. If Nina said not to worry, I wouldn't. We'd been through numerous financial crises before and she'd taken care of them. I could only trust her to do the same now.

"So, what are you going to do about Dean?"

"What is there to do? I'm not going back to him if that's what you're asking."

"Do you still have feelings for him?"

I'd asked myself the same thing dozens of times. Before his dramatic appearance I would've said no, but now? Now that he was back and still easy on the eyes, what did I feel?

"I don't know," I answered truthfully.

"And Vince?"

"I like him, yes."

"Do you see a future with him?"

"It's too early for all that," I said, even though I'd imagined myself with him many times.

"Well you better make a decision before—"

The sound of a siren blasted from my phone and cut her off.

"What's that?"

"Dean's notification tone."

"Fitting," she said, finishing off her burger.

I checked the message:

DrDoom: can we meet?

I typed "no" then deleted it.

"What does he want?"

"Huh? Oh nothing. The usual." I shoved the phone and sketch pad into my bag. "Let's go."

We left the peace of the atrium and re-entered the hectic world of NYC. Nina flagged down a cab— faster than anyone I knew, but when it stopped I didn't join her inside.

"Hey, I have to stop by the tailor's. I should be back at the office in an hour or so."

114

"Alright, that's fine. I have to make another stop too."

"See ya."

When her taxi disappeared into the sea of vehicles, I pulled out my phone, and typed:

where do you want to meet?

The response was immediate, but it wasn't from Dean.

MrParker: Hey babe, are you free?

Decisions, decisions.

The Bear Lounge of the Russian Tea Room was an eyegasm of mirrored walls and bold colors. Fighting for dominance of the space was a glass bear juggling gold spheres, and a golden tree with branches like Medusa's hair. During my first visit for afternoon tea, I was so inspired by the decor that I spent the entire time sketching instead of drinking.

"You remember this place?"

Dean's voice sounded behind me. With a waiter's assistance, he placed a tiered tray of petit fours, along with assorted jams and teas onto the red velvet cloaked table.

"I thought you might actually want to have tea this time."

"You do know that I've been here since then, right?"

He shrugged. "Not with me."

Once the table was properly set, I slid into the booth. He poured tea into glasses that resembled beer mugs then raised his up.

"Why are we toasting?"

"To new beginnings."

I could cheer for that as long as the "new" didn't involve him. I sipped the fragrant liquid then set my glass down.

"So, why are we here besides the obvious?"

"What do you mean?"

"You're cheering to new beginnings while trying to conjure up memories of the past. You can't have it both ways."

"I know, but I felt like you weren't hearing me."

"Oh, I heard you. I'm just not interested."

He reached across the table and placed a hand over mine. With his thumb, he stroked the scar that ran from knuckle to wrist.

"Does it still hurt during this time of year?"

"Mhmm," I said, withdrawing my hand.

"I still remember that day. You were so excited to go."

"Is your head ok? You were the one that insisted we go rock

climbing yet somehow I ended up with the injury."

"That's right. I still feel bad about that."

"Oh yeah? What else do you feel bad about?" I crossed my arms to keep from punching that handsome face.

"I feel bad about everything. I know I can't make up for what happened before, but I miss you, Sasha."

"So, what, I'm supposed to swoon and fall at your feet with forgiveness?"

"No, I'm not saying that. I just—Sasha, I'm trying here. I don't know how—come to my show. Just come to my show and you'll see."

"Dean, I don't need—"

My purse vibrated. It was rude to pull my phone out, but I didn't care.

MrParker: waiting for you…

Damn. I'd told him I'd be there in 30 minutes. Using the car service application, I requested a driver, shrugged into my jacket and stood up.

"Wait, do you have to go?"

"I do, but thanks for this." I gestured towards the uneaten items.

"Stay, please," he said, holding on to my elbow.

What was going on these days? For years I'd struggled with maintaining relationships, now suddenly two of the most beautiful men I've ever met were vying for my attention.

"Bye, Dean."

"At least say you'll come to my show."

"I'll see what I can do."

He let me go without further protest. As I made my exit, I smiled at how good it felt to be the one leaving.

Chapter 16

With measured breaths, I stepped through the automatic doors of First Hospital, Uptown. The competing scent of life and death always unsettled my stomach and today was no different. I focused my attention on locating Vince. When I couldn't find him during my first scan of the room, I headed to the circular desk.

The sitting nurse spoke softly into the phone receiver but acknowledged my approach.

"Excuse me. Have you seen—" I stopped when I realized Vince might not want people to know he was here. "Nevermind."

Near the bank of elevators, I prepared to call him, but put the phone back when he emerged from a door down the hall.

"Hey," he said, pulling me into his arms and kissing my forehead.

"What are we doing here?" *and how soon are we leaving?*

"Must you know everything immediately, woman?"

"Obviously."

He pulled me down the hall, smiling and waving at workers along the way. I had no clue what the plan was, but it was clear he'd been here before.

"Look alive, soldiers!" he yelled when we reached a playroom full of children. "Vince!" They yelled back. Some of them ran and grabbed his legs as he reached down to hug them.

I stood off to the side, watching him in awe.

"Who's that lady?" A little girl with freckles and long, red pigtails asked.

"That's my friend, Sasha." He smiled.

"Is she your girrrrlfriend?"

Vince looked into my eyes. "Yep."

"She's pretty!" a little boy said.

Vince laughed and stood up.

"OK, OK, guys. Go and play." The kids whined that they wanted him to stay longer.

"I'll be back soon, don't worry!" He told them, turning to head down another corridor. I was beginning to feel like a lab mouse running through a maze, but I didn't care. Vince's comment to the children drowned out all of the unpleasantness I'd felt.

117

We took the elevator to the 10th floor, walked down another long corridor then stopped in front of a frosted glass door. Vince knocked and waited for a response before pushing the door open.

"Vince! How lovely to see you, and so soon." A beautiful woman with jet black hair and kind eyes walked around the desk to give him a hug. "I presume you're here with good news."

"I always have good news, but first, this is my girlfriend Sasha Ellis. She's the designer of Sashelle Ltd. Sasha this is Gemma Varden, the Director of Public Relations for the hospital."

"Hello, pleasure to meet you." I extended my hand, trying to figure out where I knew her from. Obviously, she wasn't in the industry. Maybe we'd met at a charity function.

"You're opening a store in SoHo, right?"

"Uh, yes. We're shooting for New Year's."

"Oh, that's perfect. Now I'll have another reason to drag my husband over there!"

"OK, I'm going to jump in before this turns into a girl talk session," Vince said, placing an arm around my waist. "I just stopped by to confirm that I'll be attending the Children's Benefit and purchasing two tables."

"Awesome!" Gemma clasped her hands together. "But you didn't have to come all the way down here just to confirm. A phone call would have sufficed."

I'd said the same not long ago.

"True, but I was in the neighborhood so…"

Gemma raised an eyebrow and folded her arms.

"This wouldn't have anything to do with Juice magazine, would it?"

Juice magazine! Ah, the secret affair woman! How embarrassing. I'd over-reacted for nothing. Sure, it led to great make-up sex, but wasn't it better to know the facts before making assumptions? I'd have to remember that next time.

"You saw the article?" Vince asked.

"No, my husband told me about it, but don't worry," she added before Vince could say anything. "He found it quite funny."

As the elevator descended to the first floor, I realized two things: One, I really liked Gemma Varden and two, I was an idiot. Normally, I didn't jump to conclusions so quickly, but somehow it had been too hard to resist. Then again, there was nothing wrong with being cautious, especially when it came to someone like Vince.

"So, I guess you go there often," I said once we were in this car.

"I try."

I nodded and looked everywhere but at him, unsure of how to get the foot out of my mouth. He pushed a button and a black partition sealed the space between us and the driver.

"Just so you know I'm still kinda pissed off by your hypocritical antics."

Uh oh!

"Did I ignore you or ruin our date when you were hugging and kissing that cornball in the street?"

"Vince, I know. I—"

"Let me finish." He put a hand up. "You keep going on and on about my status affecting the relationship, but I'm always honest with you. Meanwhile you're the one whose baggage keeps falling at our feet. You're the one who keeps hiding things from me."

What was I supposed to say when he was so right?

"You know, Sasha. I meant what I said back there," he continued. "I want you to be my girlfriend, but we can't keep up this routine of me being chastised for nonsense and you kissing exes behind my back."

Heat rose to my cheeks. Was he some kind of mind reader? Did he already know what had happened?

"I'm sorry for overreacting and for not being upfront about Dean. It's just…things ended between us so abruptly. I thought I'd dealt with my feelings, but *something* is still there."

"Do you wanna get back with him?"

Considering what had happened between us, it was stupid to even have considered that an option. Still, I'd done it, and reached a conclusion. When I finally turned to Vince, a stormy blend of questions, passion, and hunger filled his expression and left a feeling like fireworks erupting beneath my skin.

"No. I don't want him back."

I thought I saw the corner of his mouth twitch, but in the dim light of the car I couldn't be sure. The voice of Carl Thomas filled the space, and I sank back into my seat.

"Is there anything else you haven't told me? Anyone else?"

I glanced at his face: dark eyes, tense jaw

"I saw him—Dean."

A bark of a laugh escaped him, but there was no humor in the icy stare he pinned to me.

"When?" His voice was hard, even.

I relayed the events of the day. I probably should've included

119

the kiss from the other night, but I knew better than to add water to a sinking ship. Several minutes passed, but he remained quiet. I peeked at his face and it was the same unreadable expression.

"Say something," I said, unable to stand the silence.

"What is there for me to say?"

"I don't know, yell at me. Curse me out. Something!" I turned to face him. We were in the backseat of a car, but the distance between us felt much wider. I inched towards him. The center console had been removed so there was nothing between us. I moved closer.

"Vince."

He turned at the sound of his name with eyes both furious and hungry.

"Vincent," I said, closing the space between us. I placed a hand on his cheek, smiling within as his expression softened.

"I am really and truly sorry...for everything. Forgive me?"

I gave my best puppy dog pout. I didn't usually stoop so low, but I really was sorry. With my face between his hands, he leaned into my body so close that I could feel his warm breath tickling the back of my neck. He caressed my face then nuzzled my ear with the tip of his nose.

"If that dude comes near you one more time I promise, he gon' catch these hands, you understand?"

I shouldn't have been turned on by threats of violence, but the way his tongue trailed from ear to collarbone and back left my brain a bit unhinged.

"Do you understand me?" he repeated, sliding his fingers from my face into the cleavage I'd so readily displayed. I climbed onto his lap and pushed the shoulders of my sweater down.

"I understand," I answered.

His face lit up and not for the first time, I was grateful for the double D cups that had hindered my ballet dreams.

Chapter 17

Vince was away for the next few weeks, but I was comforted by the fact that:

1. I came clean (sort of).
2. I was officially, officially his girlfriend.

This should've meant no worries about other women, but I was only human after all. I did a good job of ignoring the latest crop of gossip by keeping busy. The problem was those good ole', well-meaning friends of mine. No matter what I said, they weren't placated and even some of the models had joined them in their speculation.

"So, they asked Vince about his celebrity crush," Amara said, holding up a magazine as we lounged in my workroom. Well, they lounged, *I* worked.

"That's easy, Sanaa Lathan."

We all turned to Daniela who shrugged absently, "What? That's common knowledge."

My lips pulled into a smile, but I was certain it lacked sincerity. How was I going to live with everyone knowing everything about him? About us? Perhaps the key was finding new friends.

"Wasn't he in a movie with her?" Nina asked.

"Yeah, I remember that one," Daniela added as she walked in one of the new pieces. The billowy chiffon flowed like running water behind her but was still missing something. I waved her back and readjusted a portion of the side seam.

"How do you do it?" she asked, holding her arms out at her sides.

"Do what?"

"Date him. Aren't you worried he might be hiding something? It seems easy to do with the kind of schedule these stars have."

"If that's the case, then no one would know about *our* relationship, correct?"

"That's true." She nodded. "Still, it has to be hard trusting him."

"I guess, but isn't it hard trusting any man?"

"You can say that again," Nina chimed in.

I finished pinning the dress and had Daniela walk again. Just that small adjustment added more shape to the hip line and more volume to the hem.

"OK, we're done," I said.

She removed the garment and gave it back to me, keeping an arm over her bare breasts.

"Sorry if this sounds nosy, but what happened with that guy— the one with the dreads? Is he single?"

"What's up with all these questions?" Amara asked.

"Nothing, it's just things aren't going well for me on the relationship front. I figured I could get some advice or pointers or something since she seems to be happy with Vince."

The world was a strange place. Here she was, the epitome of "beauty standard" and couldn't keep a man any more than the rest of us.

"It's fine," I told them. "I am happy though I'm not sure I'm the one to take advice from. I haven't handled things as well as I could have."

I certainly had not, but there was still time for improvement. I'd start by telling Dean that we were never ever, ever getting back together.

After finishing the last adjustments and sending the models home, I stayed a bit longer to clean up the workroom. I would've liked to have the time to myself, but the girls insisted on helping out.

"I don't like that girl," Amara said, watching as Nina and I grouped several bolts of fabric into a corner.

"What girl?"

"Danilla or Vanilla, whatever."

"Daniela?", I asked, laughing, "and why not?" I asked, laughing.

"She's too nice and a busy body and talks too much."

"What's wrong with being nice?" Nina asked. "You could use a dose yourself."

"Whatever. So where are you heading tonight?"

"To a rain-check. I have other plans."

"Other plans? I thought Vince was out of town."

"He is, but does that mean I don't have anything to do because of it?"

"Yes!" They both exclaimed.

"Goodnight, you two."

To my surprise, they didn't protest further. It should've made me suspicious, but I wasn't one to look a gift horse in the mouth. The girls not asking about my plans meant I didn't have to lie about attending Dean's showcase. Telling the truth would no doubt lead to me being harangued about the virtues of being stupid and asking for trouble. Points made would ring true, but they wouldn't change anything.

Instead of going home, I used the office shower and slipped into the "Formal Emergency Kit" kept in the closet of my office: black dress, PVC and patent leather Louboutin's, diamond earrings. With neither time nor equipment for elaborate hair and make-up, I raked my fingers through my short locks then applied BB cream, a few coats of mascara and, lip stain. After a cursory glance in the mirror revealed near perfection, I called a ride and marched toward D-day.

In search for inspiration, I'd visited over half of the galleries in Chelsea's Art District and found it to be like entering the same building multiple times. Each consisted of pristine white walls, floors that resembled polished cement, high ceilings and strategic lighting. The venue for Dean's showcase was no different.

At least 200 people milled around the space, much more than I'd expected for someone whose primary medium was graffiti. Then again, the pieces at the other museum were photographs, so perhaps he'd graduated to bigger things.

With my coat checked, I accepted a glass of champagne from the wait staff and joined the crowd as they shuffled from piece to piece.

Thin slabs of concrete hung from the ceiling in various sizes and served as the canvas. Each one featured a woman in roles traditionally held by their male counterparts. Though with other men and performing such tasks as window washing and carpentry, the women were all nude.

Though done in his abstract graffiti technique, the intent of each piece was clear. How he'd managed to refine and transfer his style to such a medium was impressive. I wanted to be happy for him. Wanted to appreciate the accomplishment, but a part of me was disappointed that he'd done so much without me. Our goal had always been to achieve our dreams together.

I shook my head. Thinking that way wasn't good for either of us. I continued on, stopping to eavesdrop on the conversations of other patrons. It was always funny how two people staring at one painting could come away with such different ideas of its meaning.

Moving along, I finally sipped the champagne and nearly spit it out when I came to a picture of myself. I glanced around to see if anyone else was paying attention.

Of course they are, stupid! It's an art exhibition.

Trying to hide would only draw attention so I smiled and hoped the difference in hairstyles fooled them. Upon further inspection of the picture, I realized it was the first in which you could see the woman's face clearly. I blinked, stepped back and glanced at the previous piece—a topless, straight-haired blond washing windows. She had a scar on the back of her right hand.

I had a scar on the back of my right hand.

The slab ahead featured a female executive addressing a room full of men. Only her backside was shown, but even from where I stood the birthmark resembling Italy was visible. What was going on here? Had he really devoted an entire series of art to me? Confused, I turned back to the one in front of me. If I was honest, the piece was striking. In it, I stood inside what looked like the wooden frame for a house. Wearing only a hardhat, goggles, boots and a tool belt, my focus trained on sawing a large plank of wood. It all looked so real, right down to the beads of sweat trailing down my skin.

Stepping away, I scanned the room until Ia located a man wearing a steel blue, slim cut Burberry suit. It was sad, but I could find his body anywhere. I closed my mouth before drool slipped out and wondered why he suddenly looked so good now that I'd decided to make my position clear.

I watched him laughing and smiling like a sparkly-toothed model. When he finally noticed me, I quickly turned away.

"Hi gorgeous," Dean slid an arm around my waist. I tried to extract myself without making it too obvious but didn't quite succeed.

"Hi, how are you?"

"Much better now that you're here," he said, stroking my back. "I didn't think you'd show up. "

"Well, I admit there's an ulterior motive, but…anyway, your stuff looks great. You've really improved though I should sue you for using my image without permission." I slapped his arm and used the movement as a way to move out of his grasp.

"Please don't," he said, laughing. "I didn't think you'd mind, but hey, you really think my work is better?"

I nodded. His work had a depth that was missing before.

"So, how did you remember *everything* in such, detail?" I asked.

"How could I forget?" He smiled in a way that was his alone: Sly. Fantasy-inducing. Panty-dropping.

Using every weapon in the arsenal, I see.

His gaze roamed my body, leaving trails of lightning in its path. In response to my increased pulse, I pinched the inside of my arm. Nothing like a shot of pain to snap the body back to its senses. I continued the pinching as I spoke.

"Dean, I just came to tell you—"

"Do we have to—" he paused to greet a couple passing through then came back to me. "Do we have to do this here?"

"Here, there, what I need to say won't change."

"Please," he said, taking my hands into his. "Please, Sasha."

I don't know if it was the feel of my hands in his or the way he spoke my name—like his first and last word. Something had a miniscule voice questioning if I'd made the right decision. Something seized my mind and thoughts until all I could see was him.

"Sasha," he tightened his grip as if he'd sensed the shift.

"Sasha, just give—"

"Smile for the camera!"

I turned just in time to catch the burst of flashing light. In an instant, the trance was broken, and rational thought came screaming back into my head.

"I'm sorry," I said, dislodging my hands.

With one final hug and kiss on the cheek, I left my past behind.

Chapter 18

Tuesday morning arrived with dozens of emails regarding a damaged textile at the LA factory. After going back and forth over the phone, I decided it was best to make a trip out there. Of course, that meant last minute shifts in the schedule aka angry buyers, but it couldn't be helped.

When London and I arrived at LAX, jet-lagged and hungry, we took a cab straight to the W Hollywood. After check-in, London went to the room for a nap and I made a beeline for the spa. I was only in town for a few days, but I couldn't function without the proper massage.

The multiple jets of their shower splashed onto my body like microscopic fingers, erasing the weariness of a five-hour flight. Vince came to mind as I pulled a towel through my hair and I decided to sneak a call. Cell phones defeated the purpose of the peaceful atmosphere the spa worked to create, but they made exceptions from time to time.

After the fourth ring, I was on the verge of hanging up, when he answered:

"Hey, beautiful. How are you?"

"Good, thank you. I'm relaxing at the spa after a long flight to LA."

"LA? What are you doing out here?"

Did that worry in his voice, I wondered, but let it pass.

"I had some issues with one of my factories, so I flew out. What about you? How are the vineyards of Sonoma?"

"Man, they'd be great if I could actually enjoy them instead of—" a muffled sound cut off the rest of his words. I could have sworn I heard a woman's voice.

"Hey listen," he returned. "I gotta get back, but I'll uh, talk to you soon."

"Ok, I'll see you when—hello?"

He'd already hung up. *What the hell was that?* He didn't even sound all that happy to hear from me.

"Whatever," I said aloud. No need to let a five-minute phone call disturb the peace. I continued my day of pampering with a body wax. The pain was just bearable and provided a great distraction.

When I entered the private room, a male masseuse greeted me.

Generally, I preferred women because I could enjoy the massage instead of worrying about being groped. As the spa knew my preference, I had to assume that he was the only one available.

I had no intention of going somewhere else, so I climbed onto the table. Guy whose name I'd already forgotten moved one end of the towel just above the base of my spine, and the other just below the curve of my hips. He started with my feet, deftly kneading the tension away.

Immediately, I felt sleep knocking at the door, but I couldn't answer with a strange man so close to my goodies. I forced my lids open, but by the time he reached my thighs, I felt them closing again. They might have stayed that way if he hadn't changed his technique.

His hands went from a strong, but detached touch to a sensual, gentle stroke that warmed my insides. It was comforting so I didn't say anything…until his hands ventured a little too close.

"Now wait a—"

I flipped to my side and nearly fell off the table. Instead of wiry, blonde what's-his-name, Vince stood in his place. My first inclination was to cover my exposed breast, but he caught my hands and stopped me. A barrage of thoughts assaulted my brain, but all I could focus on was the hunger in his eyes, and the butterflies it sent swirling through my stomach.

When he raked his fingers up my thigh and pushed the towel completely off, I thanked God for Brazilian waxes.

"Wh—what are you doing here?"

"What do you think?"

"But how did you—"

"Shh," he placed a finger over my mouth. "Does that really matter?"

Before I could answer, he sealed my lips with a kiss. I thought of resisting, but it was a fleeting, incoherent thought.

I wanted to rip his clothes off, but the designer in me couldn't destroy a perfectly tailored shirt. Instead, I unbuttoned it as fast as I could and slid it off his broad shoulders. I'd seen him shirtless a few times now, but still couldn't get over having the real thing. As my fingers traversed the chiseled planes of his chest, he put his hands over mine and guided them downward.

He brought his lips to mine again and kissed the breath out of me. As soon as I managed to get his pants down, he scooped me up into his arms.

"Sasha," he breathed into my ear.

I'd never considered my name sexy until it tumbled from his lips. His fingers trailed down my abdomen then further, coaxing a sensation better than fresh-baked cookies. Better than a new pair of Louboutin's, or a little blue box from Tiffany's. When it was done, when I reached a plane I'd thought only attainable in dreams, a primal moan worked its way through my bones, through my veins. Worked its way through my lips like a battle cry. I couldn't move, hell, I could hardly breathe. I buried my face in his neck and closed my eyes. Flashes of light pulsed like stars behind my lids. Vince traced circles over the small of my back until my body calmed. "You ok?"

"Mhmm," I mumbled.

"We should probably get out of here," he said, though he made no move to get up.

"Mhmm."

His chuckle vibrated from his chest to mine. "Where you wanna go?"

"Anywhere you are," I said, because it was true.

Traffic on the 405 was at a complete standstill. Most times, it was the thing I hated most about LA, but today I was grateful for the extra time to gather my thoughts from the gutter. From the time I woke up, I couldn't stop thinking about the spa; about Vince and those magic hands.

The disharmony of honking horns brought on by impatient motorists, lifted me from my trance. We were only a few blocks away from the factory. When I arrived at building's entrance, London waited just outside the door.

"Good morning, dear," I said, following her inside.

"Good morning to you too. You look…well rested," she laughed. "How was Vince?"

Of course, the mention of his name brought images of hot oil and massage tables.

"He's fine."

"I know he's fine, but, how *was* he?" She nudged my arm.

"OK, I am not having this conversation here."

I quickened my pace to the receptionist desk. The director joined us and after a round of introductions, led us on a quick tour of the facility. I was grateful for London's presence. Somebody had to pay attention because mine kept finding its way to Vince— what he was doing, how much I missed him; how excited I was that he'd flown to LA early, just to be with me.

"Sasha!"

"Yes—sorry, what?" I turned to London.

"Are you listening?"

"Yes, yes," I said, though I kept glancing at my phone.

MrPaker: are you free tonight?

It depends on who's asking, I replied.

London jerked her head towards me.

"Sorry, I'm expecting some important info to be sent over." The phone vibrated. "See, here it is."

Mr. Parker: your man is asking.

I coughed. My man? Vince Parker is my man? I liked the sound of that.

I'm free tonight if there's a massage involved ;)

My finger hovered over the send arrow.

"Sasha!"

"Yes! Sorry." I put the phone behind my back when London appeared in front of me.

"I said, we're...

"Right. Ok, I'm coming."

I let them walk ahead a few paces before checking the phone again.

"Crap."

My finger must have slipped on the button and sent the message. It was strange. We'd had sex a number of times, but something about semi-sexting had my cheeks aflame with embarrassment. I jumped when the phone vibrated in my hand, too nervous to check it.

Mr. Parker: that can be arranged sooner...if you like

How in the world could one sentence make me so hot? Already I was salivating in places...

I read it again, intent on torturing myself.

"Ok, what is more important than the wrong dye being used for the Shakes dress?" London said through clenched teeth. Before I could react, she snatched my phone and hid it behind her back.

"I shouldn't have to tell you this, but we have work to do. This is not the time to be telling Vince how much you want his—"

"Hey, watch your mouth, miss." I put a hand over her mouth and glanced around to make sure there weren't any eavesdroppers.

"I don't know what you're talking about, London."

"Oh really." She whipped my phone out and scrolled through

129

the messages. "Right so what kind of *massage* are you hoping to get tonight."

"OK, that's it." I snatched the phone back. If we kept it up, we were sure to make a scene. "Maybe you're right, but it's not a big deal?"

"If you say so," sarcasm laced her tone. "Just remember, Sashelle is your baby. If something goes wrong, you will not blame me!"

She was right, of course, but I couldn't give her the satisfaction of knowing. It wasn't like me to be unprofessional, especially over a guy. Granted Vince wasn't just any guy. Still, company issues trumped man issues any day. I sent a final message to say I'd call him later then put the phone away.

We checked out the fabric for the "Shakes" dress. The cerulean blue we'd requested was a half shade lighter, but it could still work for what we had in mind. On any other day, I might have given them a mouthful in regard to the error, but generosity ruled, and everyone went home happy.

With all the issues handled successfully, we wrapped the meeting, headed to our car and found two waiting. I smiled at the new addition— a black Audi, and waved goodbye to London.

"Must be nice," she called after me.

Yes, it was.

Chapter 19

"Hello, Ms. Ellis. I have a delivery for you." I assumed it was the bellman. I couldn't see his face behind the stack of black gift boxes he carried inside my hotel room.

"What is all this?" I asked, following him to the living area.

"Uh, I'm not sure but I think there's a card inside…somewhere."

I shrugged, handed him a tip and escorted him out. I nearly tripped over my own feet racing to the sofa. The boxes were unmarked, so I didn't know where to start. Against my better judgment, I opened the smallest one first. Noting it was about the size of a Netbook, I carefully removed the lid.

"Oh, my Lord," I mumbled, batting my eyes to see if the name on the blue velvet box tucked inside would change. It didn't. With shaking hands, I opened it and nearly dropped the contents.

A double strand of green and white Mikimoto brand pearls with a diamond encrusted clasp stared back at me. I reminded myself to breath as I ran my fingers along their cool and smooth surface. I'd never had the pleasure of touching anything as expensive, but even more than their cost, was their beauty.

A few minutes later, when tears no longer clouded my vision and breathing resumed a normal pattern, I reached for the largest box.

After what I'd found in the first one, there was no telling how I'd react to what was here. With a deep breath, I snatched the lid off and smiled. Even beneath the card taped to the top, I could see the familiar black capital letters of Chanel, etched across the box that lay inside. It was hard to decide which one to open first, especially since this was one of my favorite designers. In the end, opening the card seemed to be the most respectful choice. I sighed, pulled it from its sleeve and read:

Sorry, I couldn't bring these to you myself…be ready in two hours!)

I set the letter aside and removed the lid. For maybe the third time in my life, I was at a loss for words when the delicate chiffon passed through my fingers. Holding the dress up, a beautiful black vintage piece, I didn't know what to feel. By the time I made it through the remaining gifts: a diamond Bvlgari watch, polka dot Christian Louboutin's and a gorgeous, croc-skinned purse, I'd ooh'd, ahh'd, and cried several times.

It wasn't the expense or brand of the items he'd given me. It was the fact that every item was absolutely "me". Which in the end, meant he had *seen* me. I glanced at the card again. Two hours to get ready, but where to? Thoughts swirled in my brain.

November…LA…ah, American Music Awards! I did a little dance inside and outside. I'd forgotten about the awards even though a few artists had agreed to wear my designs.

I showered, styled my hair and finished my makeup. With 40 minutes to spare, I stepped into the dress and prayed that it fit.

"Sasha?"

I jumped at the sound of Vince's voice just outside my door. *How the hell did he get in here?*

"Just a minute," I called, pulling my arms through the delicate sleeves. I was normally an expert at back zippers, but I didn't want to risk ruining the dress.

I opened the bedroom door to see him leaning against the wall—male model style—in a slender, ash gray suit. In that moment, I wanted nothing more than to let the dress drop to the floor, Chanel be damned.

"Hey," I said, though it was breathier than I'd meant it. His own breath quickened as he rubbed a hand over his chin then licked his lips.

"Hey, yourself."

We don't have time…we should make time…no, you have to be seen in this fabulous dress!

My mind kept up the back and forth until he placed a finger on my lips then proceeded to trace them. I clamped my legs together and forced myself not to take it into my mouth.

"Umm…"

"Umm what?" he asked, leaning closer.

This guy didn't play fair. How was I expected to breathe, let alone think when he invaded my space this way?

"Umm, can you uh, help me zip up?" Why did I feel so shy? With one hand on my waist, he tugged the zipper upward then stopped midway.

"What's wrong?" I panicked, hoping the dress wasn't too small.

In answer, he slid his fingers inside the fabric, ran them along my spine, then beneath my bra strap, pushed it down along with the sleeve. I shivered when tongue met shoulder, followed by kisses up the neck.

"What are you doing to me?" He asked, wrapping arms

132

around me. It felt good to know I wasn't the only one losing my mind. I turned and gazed up at him. "Thanks for the ego boost."

"You're welcome. You look stunning, by the way," he said, caressing my back in slow strokes.

If he kept this up, we really weren't going to make it out of the room.

"Thank you so much for everything."

"So, you like it?" he said, tightening his hold on my waist.

"I love it!"

"Good," he smiled and kissed my forehead. "I'm glad, cuz I was nervous."

"Why?"

"Because man, I've never...picked out anything for a woman before. Not like this."

"Well, you did a great job. I couldn't have done better myself."

"Really?"

"Really."

We stood quietly for a moment. He stared into my eyes as if he wanted to remember every striation of color within them. Finally, he smiled then brought his lips to rest against mine: a gentle motion that conjured images of church bells, white dresses and flowers tossed down an aisle.

The red carpet was much longer than it looked on TV and a lot more crowded. Every media outlet in the country was there. I tried my best to focus on something, anything, but hundreds of people screaming, "Vince, here!" or "Vince, who's your date?" made it difficult. I'll admit I was surprised and a bit excited when my name was called a few times as well.

Still, there was method to the madness and fun too. As I learned from our escort, Paul, the media was broken up into groups of either photographers or TV representatives. There was also a special section for fans. The photogs shouted for us to pose this way and that, while Paul constantly fixed my dress or hair to make sure it was just right for the pictures. I was just finding a rhythm when we moved on to the TV reps.

"We have to do a few interviews," Vince said into my ear.

"Huh?"

"Come on. You'll be fine."

I tried to protest, but what could I do in front of all the cameras.

With a smile I hoped said "friendly" not "crazy", I stood by his side.

"Vince! Regina from GoMusic, here," she said, leaning in a little too close for comfort. "My aren't you dashing. Who are you wearing?"

"Hey Regina. My boy Tom Ford hooked me up."

"*Good job, Tom.* So, tell me, how excited are you to be here tonight?"

His answer was lost to me as I stole glances at passing celebrities. Taylor Swift had just walked behind us, and Rihanna stood a few feet away, posing for photos. Vince squeezed my waist and I turned my attention back to the woman.

"Hello there and you are?"

Something in the way she posed the question made me want to slap the mic from her hands, but I refrained and offered her a toothier grin.

"I'm Sasha Ellis."

"Sasha E…" she mumbled the rest under her breath. "That sounds a bit familiar."

"Maybe." I shrugged. Nina would kill me for not taking advantage of free publicity. Hell, I'd probably regret it later.

"Well, Ms. Ellis, what are you wearing this evening?"

"Vintage Chanel," I answered, stepping back for her to get a better view.

Just then, Paul alerted us to move on. A good thing for Ms. So and So. She was starting to get on my nerves.

We continued down the line, stopping at a few places to be asked the same questions. I wished we could have held a sign with all the answers, but that wouldn't have made for good ratings.

"Last one," Paul announced, ushering us to a make-shift stage with yet another woman.

"Vince! Long time, no see." She pulled him in for air kisses. "And is this…. Sasha Ellis? Wow. So, I guess the rumors are true, huh?" she asked, shoving the microphone in front of me. Freezing before millions of viewers was the worst thing that could happen, but that's exactly what I did. At least I was smiling: the pain in my cheeks assured me of that.

"It's not like that. We're just really good friends," Vince said, pulling me into his side and breaking the spell.

"Really? Any chance of you guys getting together? You'd make a stunning pair."

"You'll have to wait and see."

"Guys, we gotta move." Paul stepped in.

The rest of the way was a blur of more carpet and more interviews. Lights flashed, and cheers erupted, but none of it broke through the haze of shock that surrounded me like a tourniquet. As we followed the train of celebrities and handlers entering the Nokia Theatre, I tried to swallow being "friend-zoned" in front of the entire country.

"So, what did you think?" Vince asked, plopping down next to me on the couch. We'd skipped the after-parties in favor of relaxing in his suite. I pulled my legs beneath me and tried to smile.

"It was...great."

The evening was the most fun I'd had in a while. Being surrounded by all those famous people and seeing the performances up close, was more than I'd ever imagined. Yet one small word tainted the excitement: friend. Was that the real truth? Was I just here as his Vivian Ward for the weekend?

"So, you'd do it again?" he asked.

"Again?"

"Yeah, Grammy's are in February."

"Umm, sure," I said, standing up. I could feel him watching me as I entered the kitchen: a modern, state of the art affair fashioned in sleek wood too expensive for me to know the name of. *Someone* must have told them I liked tea because they'd placed a teak box filled with a dozen loose-leaf varieties, including what I knew to be the priciest tea in the world. What I didn't know was whether to brew it or frame it...ok, not true. I put the kettle on and searched for a mug.

"You want any—oh!" I breathed, scattering bits of tea as I turned to find Vince leaning against the counter. He pulled me against his body and held my face in his hands.

"Yes," he stroked my cheek. "I want something."

I held his gaze as he brought his supple lips to mine. When his hands slid into my hair, my body ignited easily. Each time our mouths touched, I felt like a heart donor as little pieces of mine floated up and over to him.

We'd been together several times now, but the weight felt heavier this time. I was over pretending like I didn't want him. Caressing me. Filling me. Loving me.

You're just a friend, though.

135

"Sasha, what's wrong?"

"Huh? Oh nothing, I just..."

"Are you still worried that I'll hurt you?" he asked.

"No, no. It's not that. I was just...nothing, nevermind."

I stepped out of his hold and focused my attention back on the tea. Removing the leaves from their package, I placed a few scoops into the infuser. It was petty to get worked up over something so trivial. He'd invited me to go with him, so it meant something. Then again, he had also asked me to be his girlfriend so what was the problem?

"Sasha, tell me what's wrong?" He put his arms on my bare shoulders, sending a jolt of electricity through the skin. It was a bad idea to wear camisoles around him.

"It's nothing, really."

We both jumped when the tea kettle whistled as if calling foul. Vince pulled me into his arms and whispered against my ear.

"Tell me."

The fabric of my shirt stretched as the nipples beneath it hardened.

Concentrate! Concentrate! You're supposed to be mad, remember! Facing him in this condition would only make things worse...well, not exactly worse, but...complicated. I crossed my arms over my chest and waited for the perkiness to subside.

"This is going to sound petty," I said, focusing on the spilled tea leaves. "Why didn't you say I was your girlfriend?"

"Ah ha!"

A deep chuckle vibrated through my back then he turned me around. The pout on my face was immature, but I didn't hide it.

"Does that bother you?"

"No," I replied, suddenly fascinated by the chrome finish of the oven.

"I said what I said because I didn't want to share our situation without discussing it first. It's one thing for them to speculate but having our confirmation could make things crazier. I wanted to be sure you were ready."

Well...when he put it that way, my attitude was illogical. Yet I didn't see a need to drop my guard completely.

"So, *are* you?"

"Am I what?"

"Focus," he laughed. "Are you ready to tell the world you're Vince Parker's girlfriend?" he asked, pulling me into his body.

"To tell you the truth—and I know this might be hard to

136

believe—but it took everything I had *not* to tell them you were," he said, running his thumb along my collarbone. "This should be obvious, but I'm kind of crazy about you."

The words sank in and left my heart beating an erratic rhythm that would make a weak person faint. His heart beat even faster, as if racing to see who'd pass out first. Knowing how he felt should have put my mind at ease, but it only created more questions. The main one: Why me? Still, even if I didn't know the reason, it felt good to be wanted by this man.

I slid my hands beneath his shirt and traced the ridges of his abdomen.

Vince Parker is my boyfriend.

A crazy fact that grew more comforting with each thought. My hands slid up and over his broad chest.

"Take this off," I ordered, tugging at the cashmere wrapper covering my favorite mocha treat. He obliged and tried pulling me back into his arms, but I slid out of his grasp and leaned against the counter the way he had. With stripper-like precision, I removed my leggings and slid the camisole over my head, holding it in my hand.

He reached for me again, but I slapped his hands away.

"Pants," I commanded.

"You do it."

"Nah uh." I crossed my arms and waited. He pushed the sweatpants just below that sexy "V" line and I locked my knees to keep from running to lick them.

"Lower."

He laughed and pushed them down further. My fingers traced the curvature of his strong body. Placing the camisole around his neck, I pulled until our bare chests came to rest against one another. I nuzzled his nose, teased his lips with the tip of my tongue.

When he could no longer stand it: touching without touching, feeling without feeling, he lifted me onto the counter and wrapped my legs around his waist.

"Sasha," he breathed, lifting my chin until our eyes met. "Can you see?"

I held his gaze. Saw the heat, the lust; the part of him that wanted me on this counter, this floor, this everything. The intensity frightened me until I looked deeper, sank further into the depths of the brilliant brown hue until our breaths became one. I saw it then, fierce and beautiful, a fiery blaze that sought to consume me, to please me, to—

Vince captured my mouth with a kiss that could not be

137

described. It could only be felt…in my mind, in my soul, my lungs, my heart. All were marked and branded by this kiss that was not a kiss.

It was a confession.

My eyes fluttered open as fingers trailed down the length of my spine. I smiled into the pillow with a sigh, delighted that the night before hadn't been a fantasy I'd conjured up. A familiar melody echoed around us and I turned to face him, nuzzling my body closer to his.

"Do you always wake up to music?"

Vince's answering smile brightened the room. "Yeah," he brushed a curl away from my face. "It's my coffee."

He turned onto his back and brought my head to rest against his heart. I listened to its steady rhythm, lazily sweeping my fingers over his chest. Mental pictures of the last few days broadcast through my mind: the spa, the awards show, the kitchen counter. There were no words of my own to describe the way I felt, so I stilled my body and let the music envelop me.

"*It's so hard for me to say this,*" I sang along with what happened to be one of my favorite Jill Scott songs. The words tumbled out in a breathy cadence as I slid up his body until my lips came to rest against his ear. For once, I didn't second guess what I wanted to say, or wonder where I stood with him. I turned his head until our eyes ~~met, and~~met and pushed every ounce of myself into those last words.

The final note lay on the tip of my tongue, but was lost as his mouth sank into mine, claimed mine. I pulled away first, gasping for air.

"I had no idea you could sing. Why didn't you say something?" he asked, rubbing the pad of his thumb along my cheek.

"Then you *really* would have put me in the groupie brigade!"

"Hmm, I see your point."

I laughed, rolled onto my back, and tried to engrave the moment in my mind: warm fingers tracing my eyebrows, nose and lips. He pulled me back into his arms and rested his chin atop my head.

"I love you," he said.

The words wafted through the air like a fine fragrance. They stimulated my senses, faded and left me speechless.

Chapter 20

LA was a beautiful city, but I'd trade it all for the psycho cabbies, skyscrapers and freezing temperatures of NYC. I liked traveling just as much as anyone, yet it always felt good to be back on my own turf. Of course, that meant dealing with overbearing friends who thought it their life's mission to fix mine.

We're just good friends.

I love you.

The thoughts permeated my brain as I raced against Nina and Amara in a marathon to nowhere on the gym's treadmill. Nearly two weeks had passed since hearing the words, but I still couldn't reconcile them. Vince had explained his position on the "friends" matter, and I'd believed him. But the passage of time made for a wondering mind and now I wasn't sure if his love confession was real or just a way to appease me.

I increased the incline of the treadmill.

"Listen to this," Amara said, raising her voice above the sound of our pounding feet. She scrolled through her iPad and I knew nothing good would come of it.

"Everyone is buzzing about that beautiful young lady you escorted to the AMA'S. Tell us, is that your girlfriend? No, he says. She's just a very good friend."

"OK, so what's your point?" I asked.

"Aren't you pissed?"

I took a moment to think while Nina leaned over to get a peek for herself. I'd yet to discuss the conversation Vince and I had and likely never would. Amara would see it as evidence of him trying to hide our relationship. The fact that he'd been seen with me publicly on several occasions would mean nothing.

"Hey, you left out the part where they asked if he'd tell if she really was his girlfriend, and he said no," Nina amended.

"So, he still pulled a Peter."

"A what, girl?"

"A Peter! From the Bible? You know, the one who denied knowing Jesus."

"Oh Lord," Nina mumbled.

"I thought that was Judas," I said, confused.

"I can't—ya'll some heathens." Amara shook her head, turning

139

her attention back to the screen.

"*Anyway*, it's no big deal," I said. "I can't honestly say that I want us to go public."

"Well, that's probably for the best. You don't want to end up like Bennifer."

"These references!" I rubbed my eyes. "Who is *that*?"

"That was the name they gave Jennifer Lopez and Ben Affleck, remember? She had to find a "good guy" after dating Diddy. Anyway, they went on TV professing their undying love and broke up two weeks later," Nina said.

"Oh yeah, I remember. They were talking with— hold up," Amara said, fiddling with the tablet again. She couldn't do a basic yoga pose, but she could juggle an iPad and run on an inclined treadmill.

"Read this!" she passed it to Nina.

"Sources say Sasha Ellis is devastated over being put in the friend zone by actor/singer Vince Parker. Under the impression their relationship was more serious; she's now reeling over the news. What the hell?"

Sources? What sources? I'd only spoken to a few people on the matter, none of whom would do such a thing as talk to the press...would they? I scanned the other occupants of the gym as that familiar sense of paranoia set in. Everyone seemed to be in their own world, too focused on their "gym flow" to eavesdrop. Maybe they were just good eavesdroppers.

"Anyway, I think you should just dump him. There's just too much drama involved."

"Great advice," Nina said dryly. "Just ignore it, Sasha. I'm sure it'll pass with time. Now, on to more important matters. Turkey day is this weekend. What are you guys doing?"

"Ugh, I'll be in the Hampton's at my one of my mom's "look how rich I am" parties. You're both invited, by the way."

"Thanks, Amara, but I'm going to visit my Grandparents in Ireland."

"Cool. Looks like we'll all be out of town this year."

"Oh yeah? Are you going to visit your parents?" Nina asked.

"Nope!" I said, stopping my machine. They shared a glance then stopped theirs as well.

"Where are you going then?"

"Connecticut."

"And what's in Connecticut."

"Vince's family."

140

I dried the sweat from my brow, took a few sips of water and left them to retrieve their jaws from the floor.

"Did we really drive all this way to stand outside? It's 30 degrees out here," Vince said, rubbing his gloveless hands together.

"Out here" was his parent's family home in Connecticut. I was so caught up in the idea that he *wanted* me to spend time with his family that I didn't think of what it would actually be like. Now it was too late to change my mind.

"Your mom is going to hate me. We should go." I tried anyway.

"Bae, I'm not getting caught up in that traffic again."

"Ok," I said but grabbed his arm when he reached for the door.

"Wait," I straightened my jacket and pulled the wool hat tighter against my head.

"Don't worry. I promise they'll love you."

Ha! Another saying on the list of lies I'd heard before. In general, while all of the dads I'd met adored me, the moms were the exact opposite. Sure, they praised my ambitious nature, but always made me feel as if I'd never be able to take care of their son. Dean's mom was the exception.

The curtains of the nearest window fluttered, followed by a chorus of giggles.

"I think we better go in." He gave my hand a quick squeeze, but before he could touch the handle someone opened the door.

"Well, hello there," a petite woman with Vince's smile greeted. I liked her immediately.

"Hey, mom." Vince stepped inside and swallowed her up in a bear-hug. I followed, distracted from the beautiful décor by the 20-30 people dispersed through the room.

"This is my girlfriend, Sasha."

"Hello, Mrs. Parker," I extended a hand. "It's lovely to meet you."

"So formal!" She swatted my hand away and pulled me in for a hug. "Please, call me Lily."

"Yes, ma'am."

The rest of the family swarmed and before Vince could make any further introductions, two identically beautiful girls pulled me away.

"I'm Farrah or Faye, if you're lazy!" The first one said.

"And I'm Francesca, but everyone calls me Frankie. Again, lazy."

I smiled at them both and tried to find something that distinguished them. Each had thick, perfectly groomed eyebrows. Their skin was the same chocolate tone as their brother's and they each had a beauty mark at the base of their chin. Even their hairstyles were the same: a messy, top-knot.

"It's ok. It takes a while to tell them apart," Vince whispered in my ear. The next introduction was his father, a handsome, formidable man who's frame and posture suggested a military background. A hug from him was quickly followed by more from two other men—Vince's brothers—and their significant others.

I thought I had a chance to breathe when a gaggle of kids ran in. Finally, the last introductions were made, and the twins grabbed me again for a tour of the house.

"Anything to get out of doing some work." I heard their father say.

After a tour of the ground level, we stopped by the kitchen to see if his mom needed some help. Miss Lily handed me a bowl of apples to chop when I sat down.

"So, Sasha. Vince tells me you're a big-time, fashion designer."

"Umm…I wouldn't say that, but I'm getting there." I tried to steady my hands, knowing that knives and nerves weren't the best combination.

"Well, maybe you can give Frankie here some pointers."

Finally! A way to tell them apart.

"Are you interested in design?" I asked.

"Yes, yes! I'm studying at FIT."

"That's great!" I smiled, finishing up my first apple without incident. "I went there for a bit before transferring to Central St. Martin's in London."

"Wait a minute, you're *that* Sasha Ellis?"

"Umm, last I checked."

"OMG, I knew you looked familiar. I am in love with your clothes!" Frankie beamed. "I have everything from the first collection.

"You ok in here?" Vince appeared and slid an arm around my waist. I tried to shift out of his embrace, but he pulled me closer.

"And why wouldn't she be comfortable?" Farrah said. "We don't bite!"

"No, you just cut people."

"Wait, what?" I dropped the apple I'd just picked up.

142

"Hey, the past is the past and besides, it was an accident."
Farrah slapped his arm.

"What was an accident?"

"I cut one of his old girlfriends, but she snuck up behind me, so I don't see how it's my fault."

"Ah." I smiled though I was certain it lacked luster. I knew he'd had other women, but that didn't mean I wanted to hear about them. Even if they were being cut.

A few hours later, I was grateful to have made it out of the kitchen without a scratch. Grateful to have made it through the meal without making a fool of myself. Even if I had, no one would've noticed as they were too busy stuffing their faces. The food, which included macaroni and cheese, cornbread and ham, was so good that even the kids were quiet. Everyone claimed to be stuffed until peach cobbler and pecan pie were mentioned.

When no one could eat another bite, the men cleared the table and the women tackled the dishes.

"Ladies, how about a movie upstairs?" the short woman introduced as the wife of his brother asked, when we'd finished cleaning.

"Oh, that sounds great but umm…" I tucked a lock of hair behind my ear. "I think there's a game on."

A collection of gasps reverberated through the room, followed by a round of laughter.

"Lord, where did you find this girl, and does she have a sister?" his single brother asked.

"Come on, dear. You can have my chair," Mr. Parker offered, followed by another bout of laughter.

"No, no. It's her first time here so she has to come with us!" Mrs. Parker said, gently leading me in the opposite direction.

"Come on, baby! I'm sure that girl gets her fill of gossip every day plus, we need a good luck charm."

He ran a hand over her cheek before planting a kiss on her forehead. She blushed and playfully pushed him away. *Well, now you know where Vince gets his charm.*

By the time the game was over, most of the men were either drunk or asleep. Vince and the few sober ones decided to play poker, but as they prepared the table, Frankie bounded into the room.

143

"It's time for Taboo!" she yelled, waking the sleepers in the process.

"Uh oh," Vince said.

"Uh oh, is right. Pull your team together and get ready for a smack down."

"Hey, we won last time," his brother said.

"In your dreams, sir. Let's go." She clapped.

"Have you played this before?" Vince asked, pulling me to his side.

"No, but I'm—"

"You might want to sit the first round out then. It gets pretty heated."

"She'll do no such thing!" Frankie said. "You can teach her."

The rest of the women filed into the room while he explained the rules. When Frankie was satisfied everyone knew what to do, she started the game.

At first, it was tricky trying to explain words while not using those listed on the cards. Eventually, I got the hang of it and brought us within 2 points of winning the game. Our team had time for just one more card.

"Ok, this guy is a singer. Umm, an old singer who—"

"Frank Sinatra!" his mom yelled.

"No, no. He—Carlton from Fresh Prince used to dance to his songs," I said, watching the sand filter through the tiny hourglass.

"Oh, Tom—Tom Selleck!"

"Tom Sell— no, ok, the movie with Lorenz Tate and Nia Long."

"Love Jones!" someone yelled.

"Ok, take away love."

"Jones!"

"Right, now put it together, Tom…"

"Tom Jones!" His sister screamed just as the time ran out. The rest of the women leapt from the couch and rushed to give me hugs. We jumped up and down, taunting the men.

"Nice job." Vince kissed my cheek

"He's a traitor," His Uncle yelled, spilling a bit of rum on the floor. "Always consorting with the enemy."

Everyone laughed as he struggled to put his words together.

"Fo' real. How we supposedsa win if you keep bringing these girls to beat us? She even bester than that Beyoncé'—fiancée', whasser name?"

If there was a better way to ruin an otherwise perfect occasion,

I couldn't think of one. Judging by the expressions on the faces of his family—as if a priceless vase had been shattered— they felt the same.

Chapter 21

"Say something."

"What is there to say?"

Though I was the wronged party in this situation, I couldn't stop the sense of shame that clung to my thoughts like lint. A part of me wanted to scream, to demand a biography of the woman who'd zapped the energy from a room. And the rest of me? The rest of me swam in "I-told-you-so", "that's-what-you-get" and other phrases of regret conjured when the inevitable happens.

I grabbed my overnight bag from the guest room closet. My hands trembled as I stuffed my make-up and hair products inside, but I didn't care. I had to go. I had to get out before disappointment suffocated me.

"Will you let me explain?" he asked, following me.

"What is there to explain? You were engaged, now you aren't. Big deal."

"Then why are you packing?"

"You know why."

"Sasha...Sasha!"

"Don't touch me!" I said, snatching my arm from his grasp. "You're such a hypocrite. A fucking hypocrite— all this time, all this time telling me to be honest, to be upfront and look at you. Hiding a fiancé' in your back pocket."

"*Former* fiancé and I didn't tell you because I didn't think it mattered."

"Didn't think it—no, you didn't tell because you knew I would've shut you down from the start." I turned to face him and felt the anger slipping away when I caught a glimpse of his lips. I walked around him and pretended to search for something.

"Sasha, you wouldn't have given me a fair chance. You wouldn't have been able to see that I'm not like that dude."

"You're just like him!" I had to turn around now. "You're just as selfish. Only thinking about what's best for you."

"Ok, I admit I should have told you, but why does a previous engagement matter? What does that have to do with you and me?"

"Are you listening? Have you heard anything I've said? This isn't about you being engaged. It's about you being deceitful. About you withholding necessary information because it might work

146

against you." I crossed the room, snatched my phone from the bedside table and searched for a driver in the area.

"OK who's the hypocrite now?"

"Excuse me?" I glanced up.

"You heard me," he stepped closer. "That's exactly what you did. Kissing that dude, probably more times than you said. Meeting him for tea at the—"

"How do you know about that?"

"Not because you told me, that's for sure." He shook his head and paced near a chest of drawers. I tried not to track him around the room. Tried not to watch his long, lean frame stalk the floor like a predator. I failed.

"The circumstances might be different, but let's be honest, Sasha. We've both kept things from each other."

"No, I told you what was happening with—"

A light knock at the door interrupted my rant.

"Everything ok in there?"

"Yes, mom."

While he took a moment to speak with her, I went back to my phone and found a driver in the vicinity. It was only 8:15 and judging by the boisterous sounds coming through the door, they'd be up for a while. If I left now, I'd have to face whispers and pitying glances from his family. Staying meant being cooped up in a room with him and hoping I didn't—

Vince shut the door and locked it but didn't turn around. *Why is he locking the door?* My first instinct was to panic, but he couldn't hurt me—not with so many witnesses around. Then again, they were his family. He could do it and they'd all go along with it...pretend like I'd never—

"Sasha," he said, in a quiet tone that calmed the voices in my head and made me want to give him whatever he asked for.

"Sasha, I don't want to argue with you."

When he turned around, a mix of sincerity and hunger bleeding through his expression forced me to step back. The heat that gripped my body was fierce and immediate.

"I don't want to keep going back and forth about who was right and who was wrong."

In four strides he closed the distance between us, took my phone and tossed it on the bed.

"Tell me how it matters, Sasha. My past, your past—how are they relevant when I love you right here, right now?"

"Vince..." I tried to step away, but he caught me at the waist

147

and pressed me into his body. I struggled against him, but his arm was like quick-sand and grew tighter with each movement.

"I love you, Sasha. Look at me." He held my face in his hands, but I left my focus on his chest. *As if that's any safer.*

"Sasha, look at me please."

That voice again. That tone again. How could I disobey? My gaze drifted up his body, past the smooth neck, the full lips and finally met his eyes.

"I love you. Even if your brain won't accept it, you feel it here." He placed a hand over my chest, dragged his thumb across the swell of my breast. The arm at my waist loosened just enough for him to stroke the small of my back. He kissed my forehead then swallowed me with his arms.

"The question is," he breathed against my ear. "Do you love me?"

If the roof suddenly detached itself from the house and galloped down the street, I wouldn't have noticed. My mind, my body, my heart…all scrambled to make sense of his words. Where before they were like a gentle fragrance, this time the words were like anchors weighing on my heart until I had no choice but to acknowledge their truth.

But what did that mean for me? Did I love this man whose smile made me happy, made me curious, made me want? Could I love this man, knowing the baggage I'd add to an over-stuffed trunk?

"Vince, I—"

A sing-song melody ruptured the tension and made us both jumpstart. With our bodies disengaged it was much easier to think clearly. I grabbed the phone, grabbed my bag…

"Sasha, you don't have—"

"I'm sorry, but I do."

Chapter 22

"Whoa! This is nice!" one model exclaimed as we entered my nearly finished retail store. Now that the floors were in, I'd invited a few of them to check out the "runway": an abstract style "S" built into the gleaming white tiles. It was a costly addition to the space, but Nina had secured additional investors as promised and I thought the added touch would be a great conversational piece.

"Ok guys. We'll run it a few times, so you can get a feel for the layout and that'll be it," I said.

While they tested it out, I used the time to view the guest list for the opening. So far about 85% had RSVP'd "yes", which was more than I'd expected, especially since they were all from our top-tier of invitees.

You can thank Vince for that!

My heart stuttered, stopped then started again. We hadn't spoken much since his ghost of relationships past made an early visit at Thanksgiving. He was working on a film, and I had the store to attend to, so we were both fairly busy. When we did speak, the usual easiness of our conversations was replaced by curt phrases and awkward silences.

Still, I missed him. Really missed him. A fact that made me feel even more like a jerk for leaving the way I had. One day, I'd learn to stop being so impulsive. For now, I dealt with the consequences by stalking him on social media.

I pulled out my phone to do just that but stopped short when Daniela approached.

"The girls like the runway. It's different from what we're used to, but it's also fun. What did you think?"

"Looks good," I said, though I hadn't really paid attention.

"Great. I'm so excited for this show. It'll be my first in a while so I'm a bit nervous, but at least it's with someone I know."

"I don't know why you left in the first place. You were in such high demand." I slid onto one of the chairs we'd brought in.

"That was why! Things were just too crazy, plus my relationship was on the fritz so—hey, speaking of, how are things with you and Vince. I haven't seen you guys in the papers in a while."

"We're ok, I guess. Hit a few rough patches, but that's life, right?"

"Right. If it doesn't work out, there's plenty more fish where he came from."

Why did people always say that? In the first place, I didn't want "plenty more" I wanted him. Second, in the event that I did want those "fish", what guarantees were there that they wanted me?

"Well," I stood up, "the runway seems like it'll be ok, so you guys can head out."

"Alright, see you soon." She smiled.

I thanked the rest of the girls for coming and walked them out. I'd just started folding the chairs when London's heels clipped across the floor.

"What's wrong?" I asked.

"Nothing, why— oh, I'm here out of the blue, right? Sorry, everything is ok."

"Alright so what's up?"

"This came for you."

I took the black envelope from her extended hand. There was no addressee on the front.

"How do you know this is for me?"

"A messenger dropped it off; said it was urgent."

Curious, I opened it and pulled out a turquoise card embossed with a gold "W". On the back was an address, date, time and nothing else.

"What does this mean?"

"No clue, boss. You don't know?"

"Doesn't ring any bells," I said, turning the card in my hands. It was obviously an invitation, but to what I had no clue.

"Well, are you going?"

"Go where? This could be an invitation to murder!"

"Or it could be for a super-secret Alexander Wang sale!"

That might be worth the risk.

"Why do I feel like we're walking into a trap?" Amara said. I brought her along for moral support and the blade in her purse— in case it really was a trap. Judging by the nondescript residential building we'd entered, her sentiment might not be far from the mark.

I turned the card over in my hands again, anxious about what lay at the end of our adventure. At first, I'd dismissed it as an elaborate joke, but I'd always loved a good mystery and found myself unable to resist. What if it *was* a great sample sale or high-stakes poker game? *What if it was a ticket to torture?* Either one would distract me from the fact that I still hadn't heard from Vince.

"So, have you spoken to Vince yet?"

"No, I haven't and please get out of my head."

"So, you're just going to let it go like that?"

"Oh, so you care about our relationship now?"

"No, but it's obvious that you do. Why don't you just tell him the truth?"

"And what truth is that?"

"That your mother is a serial wife and you not tryna be the same."

I stared at her, mouth agape. A rebuttal formed in my thoughts but quickly evaporated. That was it, wasn't it? My hesitation in telling Vince I loved him. The reason I ran out at Thanksgiving. Denial was a bitch and so was I. I pulled the phone from my clutch bag and quickly dialed his number.

"Two more floors. Sure, you don't want to press the emergency button?" Amara asked.

"Huh? Oh, I umm, I told you, its—" my heart dropped when the call went straight to voicemail.

A soft ring signaled we'd reached the top floor and we each held our breath.

"You go first," she said when the doors slid open, revealing a narrow white hallway with only one door at the end. No sooner had we stepped out of the elevator than the doors snapped closed behind us.

"Stop jumping!" I told her.

"You jumped too."

"Oh my God, we're like two big babies. Just come on."

I put the phone back in my bag, straightened my back and tightened the sash on my jacket. We'd come this far, might as well see it through like grownups. At the door I twisted the gold handle, but it didn't open. Amara and I exchanged glances then looked around for another point of entry.

"Perhaps we should just knock," Amara said. She tapped her knuckles against the door, but nothing happened. She tried again harder, with the same result. An LED panel rested where the peephole should have been, displaying the apartment number 802 and the same scripted "W" from the card. It was a long-shot, but I passed the card in front of the panel. Seconds later, the door emitted a high-pitched beep then clicked open.

"What kind of go-go gadget shit is this?" Amara asked.

"Just come on.

When I pushed the weighted door, the soulful sounds of Normani's latest hit washed over us and flooded the corridor. Inside, thin blue lights hung from the ceiling like chains and pulsed with the bass line. On our left, patrons conversed and sipped drinks in varying neon shades.

"What is this place?" Amara asked.

"Shouldn't you know? Your dad owns half of—"

"Hello and welcome to Waves. May I take your coats please?" asked a young woman with jet black hair and a chain flowing from ear to nose. We gave her our jackets in exchange for a silver ring with black numbers etched on its surface. Guided by a track of lights on the floor, we entered what appeared to be the main area.

The same lights decorated the space except here, their variance in length and thickness gave the illusion of movement. Towards the back was a circular staircase connecting the main area to a balcony and stage. At least 200 people bounced and writhed to the booming 808 and before I could protest, Amara pulled me out to join them. I'd yet to figure out who could've sent the invitation and the more I swayed to the beat, the less I cared.

Too much time had passed since I'd had the chance to just go crazy. Tonight, felt like the perfect opportunity to free myself of all the issues that sought to hold me down. The bass vibrated through my toes. I let everything go as it continued up my thighs, caressed the small of my back and left a trail of kisses along my neck. When it wrapped a possessive arm around my waist, I opened my eyes.

I didn't have to turn to know what I'd find—who I'd find. I could smell him. Could feel the muscles I'd come to memorize in the last few months.

"Where are the rest of your clothes?" he asked, running fingers over my bare shoulders. That simple question made me want to take the dress I wore, off. I turned and clasped my hands together to keep from ripping *his* clothes off then nuzzled the palm he placed on the side of my face.

"What are you doing here?"

"Answer me first," he said nibbling my ear.

"I won't have *any* clothes if you keep this up."

"Hmm, is that a promise?"

"Mhmm."

I slipped my arms inside his tweed and leather jacket then

152

rested my head against his chest. Taking a deep breath, I did my best to add another memory to the file.

"Vince, we need to—"

"Well, hello Vince," Amara interrupted.

"What's up? Having a good time?"

"Meh," she said with a shrug. "So, I guess you're the person who invited her."

"Guilty as charged."

"What *are* we doing here?" I asked.

"You'll see in a few. Try to get to the front." He unwrapped our bodies and I resisted the urge to stomp my foot.

"Vince, wait, I really need to—"

"I know. We'll have time for that later, trust me," he kissed my hand. "See you in a few."

I watched as he headed towards the staircase in the back. When he disappeared into the crowd, I turned around to find Amara staring at me with a smirk.

"What?"

"If you don't know, I'm not telling."

"What kind of mess…"

"Are you in love with him?" she asked.

"What—I—ok, not having this conversation here. Come on."

As we maneuvered through the crowd, her question reverberated in my mind. It was the same thing I'd asked myself since hearing his confession, and I was beginning to think I didn't have an answer. After what happened with Dean, I'd stopped entertaining the idea of love and focused on myself and now I was no longer sure what it was.

"Alright, alright, alright," A male voice said over the PA system. "I'm sure you're all wondering why you're here."

"Yes!" the crowd said in unison.

"Well, let me put your minds at ease. You've all been hand selected for a first listen to the third studio album of Grammy and SAG award winner, Vince Parker!"

Women screamed, and a few men cheered as he trotted down the stairs. He hit the stage and the air filled with raised cell phones. *Thank God we moved to the front.*

I watched in awe as he ran through a few old hits before jumping into the new stuff. The crowd sang and danced feverishly, until he decided to slow things down. My heart awakened when a set of familiar, gentle notes rang out from the speakers.

Vince moved to center stage. A host of hands shot out to

connect with him, but he only had eyes for me. The words tumbled from his lips and into my heart; triggered emotions, desires and dreams I never knew I had.

"...*and if love ain't enough, I'll work to make it everything you need, show you what we could be...*" he sang, with gaze trained on me.

"Ditto."

When he finished his set, the horde around me erupted in ear-shattering applause while I stood staring at the stage like an idiot.

"Come on, let's go greet him," Amara said, grabbing my elbow and leading us toward the side of the stage. The crowd reignited when he emerged from the balcony and traversed the set of stairs that led to the main floor. The grin on my face was stupid, but I didn't care.

We forced our way through the crowd and were near the base of the steps when a woman with a familiar set of Janet Jackson-like abs floated towards him. Despite the frigid December air, she wore a tribal-printed midriff top and billowy skirt that trailed behind her like a train. I shifted my weight, suddenly uncomfortable in my drop-shoulder sweater dress and sky-high heels.

When she reached his side, fire scorched my veins as she planted a quick kiss on his lips and slid her hand into his.

"Who the—is that..."

"Daniela."

Chapter 23

Too many people in the room. Too many witnesses for me to get away with murder. Too many people blocking my path, but they'd move when they saw the flames encircling my body. What the hell was she doing here?

"I told you something about her wasn't right," Amara said, digging through her purse.

"Not now, please."

I waited for the crowd around them to thin out then made my approach. Daniela was still holding his hand. Still smiling and offering her body on a yellow-skirted platter. For Vince's part, he looked more shocked than anything, so I gave him a pass for not releasing her.

"What are you doing—Sasha," his eyes widened when I appeared before them, but he turned his attention back to her and released her hand. "What are you doing here?"

"Come on, this is a huge night. You know I wouldn't miss it," she tossed Pantene sponsored hair over her shoulder.

"Wait a minute, you two know each other?" I asked him.

"Of course. I'm his fiancée."

"*Ex*-fiancée."

The air in my chest deflated like a popped balloon. What the hell was going on here?

"Fiancée…" my gaze darted between them then settled on her. "Fiancée. Really, Daniela?"

"Wait, you already know each other?" Vince asked.

I heard him talking but couldn't wrap my head around what was happening let alone the words that came out of his mouth. I glanced up at her. Though her lips smiled, I could see the force with which she held it together. Her normally friendly eyes held a gleam of danger. Was she threatening me? Not possible.

"This is some bullshit," Amara said. "I should really whoop your ass right now."

She stepped towards her, but I gripped her elbow and pulled back.

"Did you do this on purpose? Did you seek me out?"

"Sure," she shrugged. "I had to see what you were like."

"Had to—"

155

Before I knew it, I'd released Amara's arm and slapped the smug grin from Daniela's face.

A ping signaled the next stop and awoke me from the trance I'd entered since stepping into the subway car. The metal doors moaned their way open and I stepped into the musky air of New York's underground. No matter what time, the Herald Square station was always crowded. I dodged my way through lovers, sleepy tourist, platform performers, and up the stairs into the night air.

My legs were freezing and my feet near numb. I should have gone home to nurse my wounds, but there was liquor there. And liquor led to drinking led to drunkenness led to numbness led to craving more. I had enough problems in my life without adding an alcohol addiction to the list.

Instead and to the detriment of my favorite pair of heels, I stalked the pavement that led to my office. At least there I could find work to keep my mind occupied. I buzzed myself through the glass doors, left my shoes behind and climbed the stairs.

I'm his fiancé'.

The words hurled through my mind like an asteroid bent on destroying whatever it touched. What kind of movie was I living in? It had to be a movie or prank show or something. These things didn't happen in real life.

Or maybe they did. Maybe it was Karma for all the hearts I'd broken in the past.

No. It didn't have anything to do with me. It was that crazy, deceitful bitch I'd slapped. The bitch Vince had the nerve to comfort after I left my hand-print on her face. He was probably still there now, nursing her wounds instead of mine.

"Ugh, how is this life right now?" I yelled, throwing the tape dispenser at the wall. In answer, my phone rang out. I picked it up without checking the ID

"Hello," A whisper of a voice I barely recognized as my own escaped.

"Sasha, I'm so sorry I'm—"

End call. Power off.

I flopped into my desk chair and, pulled fingers through my cropped tresses. *Sorry*. Men tossed that word around like coins in a fountain, wishing it would make up for all the pain they'd inflicted. Men were stupid.

The door of my office opened, but I didn't turn around. Only two people had the key.

"What do you want?" I asked.

"OK, that's officially the worst greeting I've ever received."

I swiveled in the chair to see Vince standing in the doorway.

"Wait, I take that back." His smile was a beacon in the night as he walked towards me.

"What are you doing here, no, how did you even get in here?"

"Oh umm, Nina gave me the code," he said, taking a tentative step forward. "And you know why I'm here, Sasha. Are you ok?"

"Yep, I'm just peachy. Thanks for asking. How's that bitch?"

"Don't be like that, she's—"

"Don't defend her." I stood up. "Do you know how long she's been working with me? How long she's been asking about our relationship. Now I find out it was all some ploy to get you back."

"Sasha, I know you're upset and I'm sorry. I really am."

The moon highlighted his frame as he moved to stand in front of me. The man was gorgeous, but I wouldn't be swayed. Though hatred for Daniela dominated my thoughts, a slice of anger was reserved for him.

How could he sit there fawning over Ms. Sexy-crop-top when I was hurting just as bad?

"Say something." He kneeled in front of me.

"Something."

He was too close. Too gorgeous. Too much for my bruised senses to handle.

"Sasha," he whispered, pulling me down from the chair and into his arms.

"I apologize."

Soft lips caressed my shoulder, penetrating my resolve.

"I see that it was a mistake not to acknowledge the pain you were feeling. You did slap the shit out of her, though," He joked, breaking up the tension. "Did it feel good?"

"Yep!"

"Hmm, maybe I should do the same to that ex of yours."

"Be my guest!"

Silence hung between us like damp laundry. I pretended to search for "something" on my desk, while my brain searched the archives for words but came up short. I liked him, maybe more than liked. But I was starting to think we just weren't meant to be.

157

When I could no longer pretend to search, I glanced up to see Vince sitting in the chair across from me, hands steepled.

"What?" I said.

"Are you ready to talk?"

"Is there anything else to talk about?"

"Why did you call me tonight?"

"Huh?"

"Tonight, before the show. You called me. Why?"

"I don't know, what, I can't just call?"

"No, not when you've avoided my calls for the past week."

Had it been that long?

"What were you going to say?"

"Doesn't seem relevant now."

He leaned forward, rested elbows on his knees. "Ok, now I gotta know."

"It's nothing," I stood up to head out then thought better of it. "You know what, no. I was calling you to apologize for Thanksgiving, to say that I was letting my issues get in the way of what was happening between us. Now, I'm not so sure."

"What issue? You said you were done with your ex."

"Not mine, my mom's."

"Wait, you dated your mom's ex?"

"No, man!" I plopped back into my seat. "I grew up with a Mom who treated husbands like accessories. She advised me to do the same, and despite my best efforts, I ended up doing almost exactly what she did. I'm sorry, I just, I don't think I'm cut out for a real relationship. Especially one that comes with so much extra."

"Finally!"

Vince stood up and walked around the desk to stand before me. He wrapped his hands in mine, pulled me close.

"Thank you for finally telling me something real. I get it now, and I accept your apology."

"Umm, I didn't apologize."

"Oh no? Guess I better get—"

"No, don't go," I said, pulling him as he attempted to walk away. "I am sorry, I—I don't know how to do this. I don't know how to forget what happened."

"You don't have to forget. In fact, remember it. Remember it enough to keep that cornball out of your life."

"Hey, I told you, you have my permission to—"

"I'd rather undress you."

"Oh yeah?"

158

"Definitely," he said, running a finger down my arm.

"Sorry," I breathed, staying his hand. "It's my turn."

I shoved my lips against his. The response was immediate as he squeezed our bodies together. Without being told, my hands discarded his clothing.

He stood up and yanked me onto his lap. Pictures. Stapler. Tape. Sketchbooks. All were banished to the carpet when he swiped his arm across the desk. Hands, warm and strong, stroked out a rhythm: thighs, stomach, breasts, thighs, stomach, breasts.

He held my face and kissed me. Slow and gentle, as if memorizing the taste of my mouth. I returned it with equal fervor. My heart still ached, but it didn't matter. Nothing mattered except the thrill of our bodies uniting.

The lights of the city blurred into a brilliant spark and climbed with me higher and higher until we fractured into millions of tiny white dots, floating aimlessly and gasping for air.

"Vince," I called his name as if I owned it.

"Mhmm?"

"I...I love you."

The words left my mouth before I could take them back.

Snuggled in the backseat of Vince's sedan, I felt like a new woman with a new perspective on love. I wasn't naive about our relationship, neither was I as jaded. Was I still upset about Daniela? A bit, but I realized it wasn't something to make him pay for. I loved him. I said it. I meant it. Finally, at peace, I burrowed into Vince's chest and enjoyed the rest of the ride home.

"Umm, what is going on out there?" he said, ten minutes later.

"Huh?"

I followed his gaze out the window and to the front of my building. At least 20 paparazzi milled around the door until someone caught site of our car. All at once, they spilled across the street. Circling like vultures, they knocked on the doors and windows, begging for us to get out. I'd seen these kinds of things on TV and in magazines but being in the midst was frightening.

"Seriously, what the hell is going on?" I asked, grabbing his arm.

"I don't know, but we can't let them trap us in here. Let's go." He reached for the door handle, but I stopped him.

"Wait, I...this is scary."

"I know, baby," he pulled me into his arms. "I'm sorry. Let's just go in quickly, ok?"

I nodded into his chest and breathed deep before exiting the vehicle. A chorus of questions erupted as we waded through. Vince's hand was on the front door when one sentence brought me to a halt.

"Vince, Vince is it true you're having an affair with your ex fiancé, Daniela Harrington?"

I looked to Vince, but his expression was unreadable.

"What—what are they talking about?"

"Let's go." He pulled me back to his side. The doorman arrived and ushered us inside while shooing the photographers away.

My legs were like Jell-O. I held tighter to Vince as we rode the elevator. Affair? What in the world were they talking about? Inside, I closed the door and leaned against it. Vince took a seat on the couch.

"So, is it true?"

"Is what true?" he stood back up. "You don't actually believe I'm sleeping with her, do you?"

"Can you just answer the question?"

"Seriously? No, I am not sleeping with her. Hell, I just found out she was in town at Thanksgiving."

"Thanksgiving! So, you've known she was here all this time and didn't say anything to me?

"Sasha, can we not go down this road again? We both know where it ends."

He was right. I knew where it ended. From the beginning I knew we'd end up exactly where we were, yet I'd ignored all my instincts. Ignored my common sense and jumped head first with no regard for what awaited below. Still, I wanted to give him a chance this time. I wanted to take the high road, but it always seemed to be closed.

"Vince, I just, this is just—"

"I know how this looks, Sasha, but please. It's me and you, that's it. I don't know what all this is about, but I promise there's no one but you," he said, holding my face in his hands.

"I—ok, you're right. I'll just—" my phone rang and kept ringing until I fished it out of my purse and put it on vibrate. Moments later, it continued to buzz against the coffee table. At the same time, several notification tones sounded from my tablet in the kitchen.

"What the hell?"

I snatched up the phone and glanced at the screen: dozens of text messages, missed calls, emails and social media posts. Vince's phone joined in the mayhem with notes of its own.

"This is crazy," I said to myself, pulling up my Instagram account to see countless photos of a younger Vince and Daniela on the beach, at the museum, at his parent's house. I stared up at him. Had that been his plan all along—to make me her understudy?

I went back to shut the phone down when Daniela's latest post captioned "Reconnections" caught my attention. They were at a restaurant or cafe and her hand rested atop his forearm, lovingly.

"What is this?"

"What is what?" he walked to my side and glanced at the phone.

"Is this recent?"

"Can't be, I only saw her for the first time at the party."

I turned to study him, but my own vision was too clouded to see a clear picture. I wanted to believe him. Believe in his word and believe in his love, but how could I when every forward step I took resulted in a setback.

"Sasha, I don't know what she's trying to do, but I swear that's not me. You have to believe me." He tossed the phone onto the couch and grabbed my hands. "I have to go take care of a few things but promise me we can settle this later."

"I don't like to make promises I can't keep."

"Sasha, Sasha don't—"

"I'm sorry, Vince. I just—I can't think right now." I finally sat down.

"I know things are crazy right now, but I can promise I'll get to the bottom of what's going on. It'll be fine, you'll see.

Chapter 24

But hours later, after escaping through the fire exit like a criminal from the throws of an angry mob, things weren't fine. I'd resisted for as long as I could, but finally gave in and searched the web. Articles from anonymous sources who claimed I was shattered by the news. Articles about the "torrid" affair between Daniela and Vince. Numerous links to Daniela's expose' on her relationship with him. In her words, they'd dated for years, but quickly fizzled once he entered the industry and was told that being "single" would boost record sales.

In a perfect world, we would've been best friends. Sisters sharing in the mutual demise of our relationship. But life wasn't perfect and like a classic Romantic Comedy, we stood in opposing roles.

I flopped into the arm chair and placed my head in my hands. When had my life become some drama filled reality how? Why did the past always show up like some unwanted visitor, disrupting life at the most unwanted times?

"So, what, you're just going to barricade yourself in here all day?"

I glanced up at the sound of Amara's voice and found Nina by her side. I wanted to be happy to see them, but considering their stance—crossed arms, pursed lips, heads cocked to the side—I knew it wasn't a social visit.

"Hey," I said.

"Don't *hey* us. What the hell is going on, Sasha? Are they telling the truth?"

"God, not you too, Nina."

"Yes, me too. Now, tell us what's going on."

With a sigh, I recounted what had transpired over the last few weeks including Vince's confession of love and the news about Daniela at Thanksgiving though at the time, I didn't know it was her.

"I can't believe you've kept so much from us," Nina said.

I glanced up at the sound of hurt in her voice and grabbed her hand. "I'm sorry, I know, it's just—I've been trying to make sense of everything."

"But we're your friends, Sasha. We're here to help things make sense."

"Are you? Because sometimes I think you just want to rub the faults in my face."

"Ok, that comment was unnecessary and a bit hypocritical. Stop picking fights with us. We're not the problem," Nina said.

"Exactly, but since we're on the topic, let me say I'm not about rubbing faults in your face. It's just letting you know when you're wrong and let's face it—you were very wrong about Vince. If you would've told that fool to beat it the minute he showed up, none of this would've happened," Amara said.

"You're right," I said

"I know—wait, I am?"

"Yes, you're right. That's what you want to hear, isn't it? That you told me so and la di da. You're absolutely right, but where does that get you or me? How does that change anything that's transpired? It doesn't because no matter how right you are, I can't go back. All I can do is move forward and if you're not interested in helping then you can keep whatever comments you have left to yourself."

I stood up and walked to the wall that held paint samples. If only life were as simple as painting. Tried a color that doesn't work? No problem., Gget another bucket and paint over it like it never happened. But life wasn't like that. It was like writing words on a page. No matter what you did, they would always be there. Sure, they could sometimes be erased and written over, but the smudges were always there lurking behind fresh ink like ghosts.

"Well, I'm leaving," Amara said. "Clearly you don't understand that none of this is about "being right". It's about you being ok. But you're a grown woman; you do what you want to do. Just please, before you toss yourself in front of a moving bus again, take a minute to think of the pain we experience when we scrape your ass off the ground."

For the second time in a few hours, I let someone I cared about walk away when I should've stopped them.

"She had a point, you know." Nina joined me as I pretended to study the blue brush strokes on the wall. "I know this situation puts you in a bad spot, but you're not the only one who gets hurt. We're there no matter what you go through. We laugh with you, cry with you, hurt with you. I'm not saying our pain compares to yours, but it hurts us to see you hurt. Especially when we know it's something you can avoid."

"But that's where you're wrong. I *can't* avoid it. I care about him too much. I—" A melody erupted from my phone, signaling a text message. I scooped it up and sighed after reading it.

"It's London. Sprightly saw a few of the articles and is threatening to pull out."

"What the hell, man. It's the weekend, plus we've already allocated those dollars to the first production costs."

"I know," I grabbed my bag. "I'll contact his secretary, but I'm going into the office to see what we can do just in case they stick with this decision."

By the time I arrived home, the sun had acquiesced to an indigo sky dotted with stars. The photogs appeared to be gone, but just to be safe I slipped inside through the back. I needed sleep. Not a few hours, but Rip Van Winkle kind of sleep where I woke up in another place and time; without all the drama of the last few months.

My mind continued the fantasy as I stepped out of the elevator and onto my floor. When I rounded the corner, I found yet another issue waiting at my door.

"Seriously, I can't deal with this right now. Why would you even show up here?"

"I know and I'm sorry," Dean said. "I just wanted to talk face to face.

"Ugh, will you ever *not* be sorry?"

I pushed past him and unlocked the door. Vince's scent still lingered in the room and brought forth the heartache I'd managed to push down. Liquid courage was the only thing that could help.

"Are you doing ok?"

"Of course, I'm ok. In one day, I went from being the next designer to watch, to that girl who got played by Vince Parker. Why wouldn't I be ok?"

I kicked off my shoes and tossed my coat onto the couch. In the kitchen, I helped myself to a mug of wine.

"I'm so—I just wanted to see you. Make sure you're alright."

"Bullshit! You saw an opportunity and thought you'd come pick up where we left off."

"I won't deny that I'd love for us to get back together, but my first priority was making sure you were alright.

"But what do you care, Dean. You committed the same crime against me and didn't look back for three years. On top of that, you have the nerve to waltz your ass up in here like it's all good. Meanwhile, you still haven't explained why you—"

"I wasn't enough, ok!"

"What are you talking about?"

"I don't—can we just..."

He plopped down onto the couch and rubbed his face. Bags sagged beneath weary eyes and the stubble on his chin appeared at least a week old. I might have noticed when I'd let him in if not for the fact that I didn't care. Well...maybe I did a little.

"When I left, I told myself it would be ok because I was doing it for you—so you could find the right person and be happy. Time passed, and I thought of you more than I should have, but I was ok until my mom sent me this."

He took out his wallet, removed a slip of paper and pressed it into my hand. After a moment of hesitation, I unfolded it to find a year-old article from the New York Post announcing my plans to open a store in SoHo.

"I read this at least a hundred times and every time, all I could think about were those nights you stayed up making patterns and turning scraps of fabric into these beautiful creations. I kept thinking that I was supposed to be here with you because it wasn't just your dream, it was our dream. The problem was I didn't know how to create and achieve my dream while also being there to support yours." He reached for my hand and pulled me down to the sofa beside him. "I know what I did was wrong and selfish, but I thought it was best to end it before resentment edged out love."

I squeezed my eyes shut and hoped it would calm the roaring tides of emotion threatening to capsize my resolve. For three years, even while telling myself I was over him, I wondered if he thought of me; if he missed me. To learn that he'd done that and more awakened a side of me I'd tried to hide.

Dean rested his palm against my face and I nuzzled it gently. So warm. So familiar and yet...

"Sasha, I missed you." He replaced his hand with a kiss. "I love you."

His mouth trailed from my cheek to lips. His hands sought my waist, found it and pulled me into his muscled body. The heat between us brought forth memories of what we were. I could see it all so clearly, the life we'd built...the love that singed anyone it touched. A fiery blazed that eventually burned us.

"Dean," I said, breaking the kiss and placing my hands against his chest.

He ignored the resistance and pulled me closer. His deepened kiss made it harder to think, harder to disregard the flames building in my chest.

"Dean, please. We have to stop."

It took a moment, but the kisses on my collarbone ceased. The groping hands relinquished my breasts yet lingered on the tops of my thighs.

"What's wrong?"

"Nothing. Everything," I sighed. "This isn't right."

He sat back into the sofa, scrubbed his face.

"For a long time, all I ever wanted to hear was everything you just said. All I truly wanted was for you to come back and kiss me like you used to. Love me like you used to." I took a deep breath and turned to face him. "It feels good, too good to know that you thought of me, but you're forgetting one thing. You didn't just leave, you abandoned me."

"Sasha, it—"

"You didn't call, didn't write. You didn't even follow me on social media. No matter how much you thought of me, missed me, wanted me. No matter how much you intended to "save" me, you spent three years not knowing whether your plan had worked."

"Sasha, I—"

"Do you know how much that hurt? To see you living *our* dream. I have memories too…the graffiti tags you did in the Bronx, your first commissioned piece in Harlem. I remember everything and every plan we made."

I paused to stave the tears threatening to jump. "But what did you do? You ran instead of giving us a chance to face whatever came. You didn't believe in us and now neither do I."

"Sasha, please. I know I hurt you, hurt us. But is this really it? Is there really no way you can forgive me?"

Could I forgive him? Could I really erase everything and start fresh? I moved to sip the wine but missed my mouth and spilled the red liquid.

"Damn," I said, trying to brush it away. "I'll be right back."

In my closet, I stared at the row of shirts without really seeing them. This day was set to go down as one of the worst in my life: played like a side chick by my boyfriend, vintage Gucci shirt ruined by wine. I tried to take heart in the fact that things could only get better.

"Sasha…"

"Ah! You scared me." I slapped his arm.

166

"Sorry, I just—have you made a decision?"

"On a shirt? Yes."

I took off the stained blouse and replaced it with a denim button-up.

"I meant about us. Can you forgive me?"

"Dean, I'm not—"

I jerked at the sound of the code being entered at the front door. "Shit!"

It was just my luck that Nina would come to check on me while Dean tried to sex his way back into my heart. I wasn't sure how much more our friendship could take.

"Be right out, Nina," I yelled, hoping it would keep her from checking the bedroom. Just as I reached the living room, the hinges on the door sighed open and stopped me in my tracks. Where there should have been a beautiful woman with lines of worry etched into her forehead, there entered instead an equally beautiful man with a storm brewing behind his dark eyes.

The human body really was an amazing specimen. While my brain pondered the numerous ways in which I could flee, I couldn't stop staring at the slim black pants highlighting toned thighs, the black t-shirt that curved beneath a smooth collarbone, all capped off by a thigh-length, gray wool trench coat.

He searched my body and I knew what I must have looked like. Flushed cheeks. Disheveled hair. An unbuttoned shirt that I quickly fumbled to fasten.

Why didn't you look in the mirror, idiot?

"You weren't answering your phone. Are you ok? I thought…"

Behind me, the sound of shuffling feet drew his attention and sank my heart. I wanted to speak, to say something to warm the cold seeping from his frame, but my tongue felt glued to the top of my mouth. All I could manage was an unsteady breath as I watched the muscles in his jaw tense then relax. Watched his fists open then close.

If the simmering tension was an indicator, I was breaths away from witnessing someone's throat being torn out. In an effort to impose calm I tried again to speak, but only managed a labored grunt resembling that of a wounded animal. Still, it succeeded in its purpose as Vince finally looked at me, though I almost wished he hadn't.

167

A pain all too familiar shone through the lines in his face, and guilt clenched my heart.

"Vince, I—"

"Keep it," he said, turning back the way he'd come.

"Wait."

There was no way I'd make the same mistake again. I followed him down the hall, grateful to be the only tenant on my floor.

"Vince please. Don't leave like this."

"What should I do, then? You keep swearing nothing is happening with—nah, you know what? I'm good. It's obvious you can't let go of that cornball ass dude so I'm good. Do you."

"It's not like that." I blocked his path. "We were, he was just telling me—"

"Do I look like I give a shit what that dude has to—this is funny." He paced in front of me. "You chewed me out over my past, but every time I turn around you're begging me to understand yours. I'm done with this shit."

He slid me to the side and pressed the call button on the elevator panel.

"Hold up man, you can't talk to her like that." Dean suddenly appeared.

"No, Dean its—"

"Yo, I suggest you mind your fucking business before you get dragged down this hallway."

"What? We can do whatever—"

"No, you cannot." I wedged myself between them. "Dean just leave, please."

"Sasha, I can't leave you with this dude while he's—"

"I'm sure he won't hurt me any more than you did."

"Sasha…"

"Bye, Dean and please, do not contact me anymore."

When the elevator closed on him, I hoped it was for the last time. Vince jabbed the down button.

"I know you're upset right now, but please don't leave like this. You said you wanted to talk so let's talk," I pleaded.

"That was then, this is now. Keep whatever bullshit explanation you're about to give. I'm done."

"But Vince, nothing happened."

"Really? Have you seen yourself? You're standing there with your titties out and you're gonna tell me nothing happened?"

I grasped for the right words, but they were just out of my reach.

"Exactly."

He turned to the elevator and continued to jab the button as if that would make it come faster.

Wrong. Everything was all wrong and I couldn't think of anything to stop the wall growing between us. The steel doors hissed open and he stepped inside.

"Vince please. I...I love you," I stepped forward, hoping he saw my sincerity. *Felt*, my sincerity.

"Nice try, Sasha, but that's not enough."

Chapter 25

The fall-out from our break-up was much worse than I'd expected. I spent over a week at Nina's place dodging paparazzi, searching for another model, and ensuring investors that the scandal wouldn't harm the business. I was right, of course. The usual fascination with celebrity drama spurred the public's response and as more people learned who I was, the harder it became to keep clothing from my line on the shelves.

I knew I should've seen the influx of sales as a positive, but I couldn't help feeling resentment as they capitalized on my grief. Still, as the public's interest died down, I obsessed over the printed details more and more and realized it wasn't some random source providing conjecture. Someone was feeding them the truth, with details only I or those close to me might have known.

I stood in the window and stared over the concrete buildings dotting the skyline. If I fell, I was certain the pain would be just as bad as the unavoidable conclusion I'd come to in the last few days. The only thing Dean would gain through leaking the information was embarrassment. The same was true for Vince which meant only one other person could have done it.

"Good morning. Sorry I'm late. The stupid train had issues again and—"

"It doesn't matter."

London stood just inside the doorway with windswept hair, rosy cheeks and a red nose. She must've walked the majority of the 10 blocks from her apartment.

"What's going on?"

"You're done here. Sorry I couldn't catch you before you came in but pack up your stuff. I want you out by noon."

"Wait, what? What are you talking about, Sasha? What's going on here?"

"You're gonna act like you don't know?"

"Who's acting? I just walked in the door and you're firing me."

"I know you're the one who told the press."

"Ok, now you've really lost me."

"How else would Juice magazine know about my involvement with Dean? About our past and current…indiscretions. About the ins and outs of my relationship with Vince."

"You're joking, right? First of all, why would I ever do that and second, am I the only person who knew what was going on? Have you questioned any of your other *friends* about this? Because if you haven't, you—"

"They would never do this to me. Now, please collect your things and go."

I took a seat behind my desk and rifled through the papers on my desk to signal the end of the conversation. For a moment, I almost believed her feigned innocence at the suggestion of being the perpetrator.

"Sasha…"

"Gguh jyuh! Get out!"

London's sharp intake of breath brought my attention back. Tears welled in her eyes and as she turned to leave, I wondered if I'd gotten it wrong.

With London fired and Nina out of town, I'd spent all day fielding calls, accepting last minute deliveries and merchandising items for the mini collection. In 72 hours, everything I'd worked for would culminate in the opening of a flagship store. But for now, all I wanted was to collapse into a foaming tub of hot water.

I'd barely taken 10 steps into my apartment before my phone rang. Whoever it was had to wait. I peeled off my clothes and tossed them on the bed. In the bathroom, I added soap and water to the tub then sprinkled aromatic beads over its surface. Minutes later, the fragrant smell of toasted coconut filled the air. I submerged my body in the warm liquid. As it eased the tension from my muscles, I couldn't help wishing the soft waves lapping against my skin were Vince's hands. His fingers caressing my body, making me hotter than the water ever could. Were we really over? If so, someone had to break it to my heart.

The bath refreshed my body but did nothing for the thoughts of Vince orchestrating a hostile takeover of my brain. Nearly three weeks had passed and he'd yet to return any of my phone calls. I tried my best to apologize but couldn't be sure if text messages conveyed my sincerity. I wanted to see him. *Needed* to see him, but as that wouldn't happen any time soon I'd settle for the next best thing: a good book with a side of liquor. I pulled on a new t-shirt and shorts and headed for the kitchen.

On the way, the phone rang out from my purse. I ignored it and proceeded to fix a glass of raspberry lemonade with coconut vodka. Drink in hand, I headed to my room only to be stopped by the bells of the phone. That kind of persistence could only be one person. I stomped to the couch and retrieved the device from my bag.

"What is it, Nina?"

"Why are you dodging my calls?"

"Nina. What do you want?"

"For you to turn off that attitude and turn to NBC," she instructed.

There was no use arguing with her, so I did as I was told. Sitting cross-legged on the sofa with the phone in the crook of my shoulder and sipping absently, I turned on the TV just as Jimmy Fallon launched into his monologue. It was always fascinating how comics could make a joke from just about anything.

After several guffaws from the audience, followed by a few brain-numbing commercials, Jimmy was back in his seat and announcing his first guest: singer and award-winning actor, Vince Parker.

"He looks good!" Nina pointed out.

"Uh huh."

I knew I missed him, but I didn't know how much until the moment he walked out on stage. He looked stunning in a charcoal grey suit, tailored to perfection and a lavender shirt. His hair and goatee were newly trimmed, and his large brown eyes sparkled when he smiled.

Not one bit of their conversation registered in my brain as I sat distracted by the shape of his lips. Several minutes must have passed before I noticed their playful banter had come to a halt. With a shy smile, he rubbed the back of his neck which meant he was nervous about something. I leaned forward attentively, hoping they'd repeat whatever it was.

Jimmy waited for the crowd to calm down before speaking, "I hate to be the guy that gets you on national TV to ask what happened, but...what happened?"

Vince hunched his shoulders and sent a ripple of chuckles through the crowd.

"Come on, you gotta give me something. The ladies are dying to know if you're really single again. Right, ladies?"

On cue, the women in the audience hooted, hollered and clapped. I sucked my teeth and sipped the drink. *Single.* Was he single? Was I single? It didn't feel like we were over. By now I was damn near in front of the TV as I waited for Vince to respond.

"Why couldn't Jimmy play some idiot game with him, the way he does with all his other guests? Why pick now of all times to be serious?"

"Shh!" she warned.

The audience was quiet again. Vince crossed his leg and ran his tongue across his bottom lip.

"Well, Jimmy the truth is—"

I turned the TV off. As much as I wanted to know how he felt, I couldn't stomach being rejected in front of millions of viewers. If there was anything left between us, I wanted to find out face to face. If that was even possible.

"Oh my—did you hear that?"

"No, I didn't. I turned the TV off."

"Why would you do that?"

"Because, Nina. Whatever he has to say, I want him to say it to me, not Jimmy or America or any other media outlet."

"Are you sure, because he—"

"Bye, Nina!"

"1, 2, 3!"

I opened my eyes and clapped a hand over my mouth. The store was everything I'd imagined and more. Sky blue fixtures with silver accents. Lucite chandeliers that dripped like icicles from the ceiling. Alabaster marble floors shining like crystal. And clothes. My clothes. Hanging in a plethora of fabrics and begging to be touched and taken home.

"Well, what do you think?" the project manager asked.

"It's—I love it."

Only one thing—one person could make the moment perfect, but I'd slowly resigned myself to the idea that we really were over. I'd fully expected a call from Vince after his talk show appearance, but the silence between us continued.

All seemed lost on that front, but at least there was one glimmer of good news within the rubble. Our "high-profile" break-up put me on the radar of some well-known Supermodels. I'd gone from having no feature model, to having a choice between the best of the best. Again, good news, but not what I really wanted.

The manager showed me the rest of their work: the hand-carved register shaped like an S, the floating staircase leading to an office and private showroom. When the tour was over, I continued on my own inspecting each style on display and rearranging any that felt out of place. The mannequins in the front window still needed outfits, but I couldn't decide what to put on them. I grabbed a few styles and tried them out, but nothing worked.

"Ugh, this is annoying." I marched to a nearby rack and returned several dresses.

"Maybe you should create a few pieces just for the opening."

I jumped at the sound of London's voice. A smile tugged at the corner of my lips until I remembered we weren't speaking.

"What are you doing here?"

"I came to talk to you."

"I've said all I need to say." I headed to another display and grabbed a skirt and blouse.

"You did, but I didn't."

"Listen London, I don't have time for this. The opening is—"

"Don't give me that shit, Sasha. I know very well when the opening is. I'm the one who suggested the date. I picked out the mannequins you're fussing over. I'm also the one who placed the final orders for all the fixtures, light bulbs, paint colors, doors and--"

"What's your point?"

"My point is I put just as much heart, sweat and time into this place as you did and for you to think I'd ruin it by mouthing off to some reporter is hurtful to me and stupid of you."

"Now wait one—"

"No, you wait. Did you even ask any of your friends if they had something to do with it? If you had, you might have been surprised at their answers."

From her purse, she pulled out her phone then passed it to me. "Take it."

I hesitated for a moment then grabbed it.

"Push play."

I followed London's instruction and pressed the triangular symbol over the video. A burst of laughter erupted from its tiny speaker followed by a familiar face that sunk my heart:

"I promise, it's true. Dean is her ex-fiancé. She still has feelings for him, so I don't know how she'll handle the situation with Vince. I think she likes him too, though.

"Wow, this is crazy, but let me ask you something."

"Go ahead."

"You're her best friend. Why would you come forward with something like this? Did she put you up to it?"

"No, no, it's nothing like that. I just thought this was a great opportunity to drum up business for the brand."

"It seems like she—"

I stopped the playback. If I had to make a list of all the people in the world who could betray me, Nina's would never have crossed my mind. Yet here was indisputable evidence that she'd done just that. *Business for the brand.* Is that what my heartache amounted to? What our friendship amounted to?

"Where—where did you get this?"

"I asked my contact at Juice to look into it. Apparently, Nina got in touch with the gossip columnist shortly after Dean came back and has been feeding her info ever since. She didn't know she was being filmed."

Knees weakened as I held back tears. I dragged myself to the window and slumped down amid the dismembered mannequins. Was this really my life? A former fiancé crawling back only to ruin the best relationship I'd had. Countless production issues nearly sabotaging my life's dream. Firing the best assistant I'd ever have, only to learn my best friend was behind the tabloid fodder. When would this foolishness end?

"Are you ok?" London pushed a plastic leg aside and sat down with me.

"I don't know."

She nodded and placed a soothing hand on my back.

"If it's any consolation, I don't think she did it maliciously. You know how she is about the company's *bottom line.*"

"Ok, but that's no excuse. This is my life…"

"I know. Just talk to her alright? Don't do what you did to me. Give her a chance to explain."

"Umm, about that…"

"I'm waiting."

"Mian he. Really, I'm so sorry."

"You should be." She pinched my arm.

"I know, it's just—I never thought…"

"Neither did I, but it'll be ok."

"Will it?"

"Only if you unfire me, up my salary by 10% and give me an extra two weeks for vacation. You know, for pain and suffering."

"Done."

"Done? Damn, I should've asked for more."

Like a stalker, I stood within the shadows of Vince's building.

I'd made the last phone calls. Sent the goodbye messages. I was supposed to be done. If it were some other man, I might've resisted and held on to the pride I had left. But I needed him. Needed someone to fill the void made deeper by the betrayal of my best friend.

It didn't help that Daniela admitted the photo she'd posted was old. The sleuthing powers of my social media followers had forced her hand, leaving both of us with apologies to make. I just hoped I wasn't too late.

Propelled by the thought, I flipped the collar of my jacket up and entered the lobby.

"Ms. Ellis, how lovely to see you again," the doorman said. "You haven't come to see us in a while."

"Hello." I tried a smile. "I've been a bit busy lately."

"Ah. Well, I'm sure Mr. Parker would have loved to see you."

"He's not here?"

"No, he's not."

"Any idea when he'll be back?" I asked

"No, but I'll tell him you stopped by."

I contemplated going up to wait until he came back, but decided I wasn't quite that desperate. With nothing left to do, I pulled the coat tighter on my body and headed back into the chilly evening. A gust of wind greeted me when I pushed through the doors, but it wasn't the reason my legs stopped their forward motion. It wasn't the reason my feet stuck to the ground like a tongue to a frozen pole.

It was the familiar black Audi parked at the curb. No, not the Audi. The long, toned legs emerging from the open door. The frame that spoke of spinning classes and 5am workouts, clothed in an ash gray sweater dress and magenta trench coat. The temperature hovered around 30 degrees, but no one told the sweat as it beaded on my neck.

I wanted to run. I wanted to grab a fistful of her hair and drag her up the sidewalk. I wanted to give in to all the violent images my brain suggested, but my feet were still stuck. They tingled in my Ferragamo pumps as he...Vince...*my* Vince, closed the door and helped her onto the sidewalk.

Another gust of wind prompted me to turn away, but I couldn't. I just stared at them—smiling at each other as they babbled about something stupid. The more I stared, the more confused I became. Without question my hatred for her was instant yet how could I fully hate someone dressed so well?

The battle in my brain was quickly resolved when his eyes met mine. Was that surprise in his slackened expression? Guilt that halted his steps? I wiped my eyes, intending to step towards them. My feet had other plans. They took me in the direction I'd come, towards a cab parked conveniently at the corner. Footsteps quickened behind me. My name was shouted on the wind, but I walked faster and slipped into the cab.

"Sasha!" Vince banged the window like some repentant lover in a Romantic Comedy. The cabbie saw his drama and raised him with a screeching exit. In the backseat, I wilted into the wrinkled leather and sped off towards the sunset.

Chapter 26

A pile of crumpled sketches littered the floor of my office like crumbs. I grabbed a new, sharper pencil and started again: head, narrow shoulders, slender torso.

"Ugh!" I balled it up and added it to the team on the floor. I couldn't get my mind straight. For three hours, I'd tried everything I could to purge the pictures from my brain, but they seeped from my dreams and reappeared as toned, trench coat wearing croquis. How had Vince moved on so quickly? Obviously, there were a number of willing participants just waiting to be put in the game, but I didn't think *he'd* be ready to suit up so soon. Then again, why was I surprised? From the start I knew he'd never really be into me.

"What happened? Were you playing waste paper basketball again?"

I glanced up at Nina's tooth baring smile that left crinkles at the corners of her eyes. For over 15 years, that smile comforted me more times than I could remember. Now I wondered just how many of them were real. How many of them held secrets?

"So, what's going on? Were you able to hold up the fort without me?"

"I always do."

"O…kay." She stepped through the balls of paper and towards my drafting table. I went in the opposite direction and took a seat at my desk. Everything I'd planned to say felt stupid now. I felt stupid for trusting her all this time. Still, pretending I didn't know would only make the impending fight worse.

"Hello? Earth to Sasha."

She stood in front of my desk, one hand on her hip. "Is something wrong?"

"I don't know, Nina. You tell me. Is there something wrong?" I leaned back in the chair and crossed my arms. Heat rose through my chest as I watched her expression slip from inquisitive to confused. The longer she took to answer, the further the warm sensation spread until…

"I should punch you in your face, right now!" I leapt from my chair. "How can you stand there like you don't know what you did?"

"Sasha, I—"

"Sasha, what? Are you gonna say you don't know what I'm talking about?"

I pulled the video up on my phone and pushed play. The color drained from her face when her voice filled the room. She brought a hand to her mouth just as a tear slid over her pale cheek. I'd rarely seen her cry and a twinge of guilt pinched at my heart, but I quickly pushed it down. This was her fault.

"Sasha, I'm so sorry…I—I can explain."

"You can, and you will."

She eased into an arm chair and wiped her face. I stayed behind the desk to maintain the barrier between us.

"I didn't intend to hurt you."

"Why do people say that like its true? You knew your actions *would* hurt and you did it anyway. How is that not intentional?"

"It's just…we were having financial issues."

"So now you're going to lie too? This isn't—"

"I'm not lying. I should've told you sooner, but I was sure I could handle things on my own. When Ardene group pulled out, I couldn't find anyone to replace them. We were so close to our dream, so I—"

"You decided to play me."

"No, it wasn't like that. The first few stories weren't me, but I saw the attention—the sales boosts we got, and I figured it could help. New orders were coming in like crazy. I was able to charge more and make them pay up front. Plus, Juice paid a huge amount for the story…I just wanted to make sure—the opening was so important, I…"

"So, I'm supposed to be ok with this because you did it for the company?"

"I know how much the store means to you, I just—"

"The store? What about my life? My sanity? Our friendship? Do those things mean nothing? If you really wanted to help, you should've come to me. I could've talked to my step-father and if all else failed I would've begged Amara to talk to her father."

"Your dad has already done so much, I didn't think…and Amara. I never thought you'd consider that."

"You never gave me a chance to, Nina. You, of all people know how hard it was for me after Dean left. You knew I was having a hard time reconciling those old feelings and moving on with Vince. You knew everything, and you put it all out for the world to see and criticize. Good intentions or not, you—I don't know. I just—I think you should go."

"Go?" she stood up. "What do you mean?"

"I mean you should leave. I don't want to see you right now, and don't—I don't want you at the opening."

"Don't want me—don't do this, Sasha. We worked so hard for—"

"We? This is *my* dream! *I* worked so hard. I worked my ass off for this. I stayed up all night making patterns and sewing 'til my fingers bled. I moved thousands of miles away from my family to get the best education I could. I sacrificed my relationship for this. I lost the love of my life for—"

Fingers trembled at my sides. Silent tears burst through the barrier of my lids. I didn't know whether to slap her or run from the room. In the end, I walked to my desk chair and collapsed into its waiting arms.

"Sasha, please. I know it was wrong, but can you—"

"You know the sad part in all this? You couldn't tell me yourself. When I came back after Thanksgiving, I stayed at your house for a week. For seven whole days I was there, stressed out and crying and what did you do? You tried to dig out the knife you'd placed in my back by telling me it would be ok."

"Sasha…"

"Just stop, ok? I don't wanna hear it."

I turned to my computer and scrolled through whatever came up on the screen. She stood at my desk for a few more minutes then left. No sooner had she disappeared from view than the tears restarted. I let them flow. Let the sobs rack my body as I cried for past hurts and present disappointments.

The last few months were the hardest of my life which meant things could only get better. I thought back to the beginning of my dream. Before regretful fiancés. Before a certain gorgeous celebrity and a traitorous, best friend. With a few calming breaths, I dried my face and eyes then went back to the drawing board.

The day had come; the culmination of years of hard work, late shipments, incorrect fabrications, factory changes and worried investors. Every bit of drama had been worth seeing the pastel blue Sashelle Ltd. sign, glowing above the door. Guests representing both the fashion and entertainment worlds mixed and mingled as models clad in my latest designs, stalked the abstract runway to the pulsating beat of Electro-pop. I smiled at the scene though a tinge of sadness gripped my heart.

"How does it feel to see your hard work pay off?" Amara said above the music.

She'd pulled her tresses into a top knot and clothed her petite frame in a teal, lace pencil dress from my fall line.

"You look great!" I kissed her cheek. "And this is...great."

That was the only thing I could say to explain the overwhelming feeling of accomplishment. There was only one thing that could make the evening better...well, perhaps two things.

"Cheer up. I told Nina to come."

"But I didn't need—"

"Hey, your parents are here!"

I followed her pointing finger to see Karen beaming as her bodyguard—aka my dad—kept a firm grip around her waist while guiding her through the space. If I were him, I would've done the same. Dressed in a tea-length, black sequined gown, she could have easily been one of the models moving through the horde of people.

"Ooh, Karen you look good." I kissed her cheek and twirled her around to get a better view.

"Tell me about it. I almost had to lay one of these young boys out—jumping out of nowhere asking if he can buy her a drink," my Dad said.

"Hush, Phil. At least you know I still got it."

"Yeah, and *it's* all mine."

He pulled her in for a gentle kiss on the forehead. Over 30 years of marriage and they still shared the spark of Newlyweds. I only hoped I could find someone who treated me just as good as he treated her.

You did.

I did. I'd found someone and pushed him away.

"So, where's Nina?"

"Huh?"

"Nina. She's coming right?" Karen asked, pulling me off to the side.

"We talked about this already."

"Yes, and I was under the impression that you'd changed your mind."

"That's because you *wanted* to be under that impression."

"Listen, I know you're upset, but you know she would never hurt you on purpose. That girl has been one of the most constant things in your life. She's been there for you in all those times we couldn't, and I'm not going to let you throw away that kind of

181

friendship over some mess."

"But it's not mess, it's—"

"There they are!" Amara dashed off.

"It is a mess!" Karen continued. "You had no business meeting Dean in the first place. And don't give me that mess about "closure". You kids and your excuses. If you close the damn door, it's closed."

"Karen—"

Just then, Amara reappeared with London and Nina at her side. The three of them shared a glance before Amara nudged my arm.

"Relax. You know you wanted her here, anyway."

"No, I didn't," I mumbled, half-heartedly.

A twinge of pain nibbled at my heart, but I let it pass.

"Hi," Nina said.

"Hi."

"Oh, come on you two. Make-up already."

I glared at London, but she didn't back down.

"What? I know you're pissed, but this night belongs to *both* of you so—" she clapped her hands, "apologize to each other and let's move on."

She'd wait all night before I uttered a word that even sounded like apology.

"It's ok, London. It was a mistake for me to come. I'll just— bye." Nina turned and headed towards the front doors.

"Sasha! Don't let her leave like that," Karen interjected.

"Seriously," London said. "What she did was messed up, but you can't deny it helped us out. Look at all these people."

It hurt to admit, but London was right. The guests in attendance far surpassed the original list we'd created. Not long ago I'd dismissed the public's infatuation with the demise of my relationship, but I couldn't ignore the attention it brought to the brand. Was it really so bad to give a bit of myself to insure the success of the company? I'd been doing that for years, already.

"Ugh, fine!"

Due to the ever-growing mass of people and the fact that many of them stopped her to chat, Nina didn't get very far. I suffered the same fate and after exchanging a round of pleasantries with several Bloggers, I caught her by the arm and pulled her into a nearby fitting room.

"Don't think I want to be in here. Karen made me," I folded my arms.

"Yay, Karen?"

"Whatever. And don't think this is going to be that easy. You hurt me, Nina."

"I know and I'm—"

"If you say sorry one more time, I'll hurt *you*."

"Ok, sorry—ooh, ow!"

I pinched her arm. She bruised easily so I knew it left a mark. At least she'd have a reminder. Outside, the music died down and London's voice traveled through the PA system.

"This isn't over. I haven't forgiven you yet, but obviously we don't have time so…"

"So, you can curse me out—again, later," Nina said, pushing me out the door.

A swarm of cheers enveloped me as I headed to the center of the runway. When the voices and applause settled, I took a deep breath to keep the tears at bay.

"Wow! Where to begin?" I pulled fingers through my hair to buy a bit more time. "This has been a dream of mine since I was a little girl and I'm so grateful to everyone who helped make it a reality. As you probably know, this has been a pretty *eventful* year for me."

Chuckles rumbled through the room

"I wouldn't have made it through without the best assistant ever created—London Park, and my best friend and business partner, the beautiful, Nina McCullough."

The crowd clapped and cheered for them, but my attention was suddenly snatched by the man walking through the glass doors. My pulse quickened and prickles of sweat formed in my palms.

"Thank you everyone for coming and here's to the next opening!" I lifted my glass of champagne, took a sip and quickly stepped down into the arms of my smiling family. Nina was last in the round of hugs and I squeezed her harder than anyone else.

"What is he doing here?"

"Who?" she pulled back and looked around.

"Oh. I invited him. Didn't you—"

"You invited him? You're not even supposed to be here."

"Hey, that was a rash, last minute decision on your part and anyways, does it matter? You want to see him, don't you?"

"No," I pouted.

"Ok. I'll just go tell him to leave."

"No!" I grabbed her before she walked away.

183

"So, go talk to him."

I resisted the urge to stomp my foot, and instead snatched another glass of champagne from a server passing through. Thoughts floated through my mind like specks of dust. Back and forth, they teetered between putting him out and jumping into his arms with one directive: take me away. It didn't help that his suit—black, slim-cut, with thin lapels—fit him to perfection.

"Hi," was all I could say when he reached me.

"Hey."

He stepped closer and wrapped me up in a hug. The warmth of his embrace reminded me of home. His scent brought back too many memories. I reached up to plant a kiss at his neck but was stopped by visions of a shapely woman stepping out of his car. I stepped back, and he pulled me closer.

"Sasha…"

My name was like a surge of electricity on his lips. It shocked my senses as it zipped through my veins, igniting every emotion I'd tried to extinguish.

"You haven't answered your phone, so I haven't had a chance to—"

"Stop." I pushed away from him, this time without resistance. "There's nothing to explain. You've moved on and…that's that, I guess."

"Is that what you—?"

"Vince! I've been looking for you. We need to—oh, hi."

I had the strongest sensation that I'd experienced this moment before. Someone I'd loved, correction: *I love*, being pulled away by a woman who couldn't be more different than me. In this case, a goddess with ivory skin, flaxen hair and a blush-colored sheath dress that hugged every curve of her body. The same fashionable woman who'd pervaded my thoughts for the last few days.

"Good, you're here. Sasha, this is—"

"Wow, just…wow—"

The sentence fell like the tears I couldn't let them see. Why was this happening to me, again? Had a really stacked up this sort of Karma? I pushed through the crowd, hoping my smile read "happy" as opposed to psycho. In the fitting room once again, for an entirely different reason, I cried. I should've been angry that he'd had the nerve to bring her here. Angry that she'd smiled so brightly upon meeting me. I might've been furious had it not been for the blade working its way through my heart.

I leaned onto the mirror. Watching myself cry was more painful than actually crying. I turned around and leaned against it, welcoming its cool surface as I stared up at the ceiling. The music caught my attention first. The keyboard. A quick succession of notes that tugged at a memory: *Lips against his ear. Hand on his chest. My voice—no, not mine...Vince's voice, singing of the struggle in finding the right words.* No, that wasn't right.

A roar of applause erupted, and I eased out of the fitting room, leaning against the frame for support. He stood at the edge of the runway beneath a haze of light. Microphone in hand. Gaze searching, searching until it found me. Caught me.

"I think it's better that I tell you now..."

Without any directives, my feet moved toward him. His song left the guests in a happy trance, broken only when I tapped their shoulders to pass.

Our eyes never parted. Not when I reached the stage. Not when he knelt down to take my hand.

"I won't let you...go."

The final lines poured from his lips. Poured from his heart like rain in an attempt to dissolve every doubt, every negative thought, everything that meant nothing. My resolve melted and dripped like wax as he hopped down and pulled me into his arms.

With the spell broken, the crowd erupted in cheers before turning to their phones—likely creating a viral sensation of his performance. I could only stare into his eyes, brimming with a passion that heated my insides.

"Forgive me."

He kissed my forehead.

"Trust me."

He kissed my eyelids.

"I love you."

Spontaneous combustion. It was the only way to describe his lips against mine. Hands caressing my body. I missed him and yet...

"Vince, I—"

"Vince, Sasha, wow! Why didn't you tell me you were going to do this?" Ms. Leggy-model-type made another appearance. *How did she know my name?*

"I could've had someone here. Either way, I'm sure plenty of video was captured. This is going to be great. We can use this for—"

"Alright, alright. Let me stop you right there. Sasha, this is Laurie Paulson—my new Manager and Publicist. Laurie, this is

Sasha."

"So nice to finally meet you." Her smile brightened as she shook my hand. "I wish we could have met the other day, but I understand you had to get back to this fabulous place."

"Uh, yeah." I nodded.

"I had to let Carter go," Vince explained.

"Really?"

"Yeah, but I didn't come here to talk about that. Laurie, excuse us please."

"Ok, ok. TMZ is outside so make sure they get a good shot when—"

"Laurie…"

"Right. Nice meeting you, Sasha." She smiled and teetered away on shoes I'd love to add to my collection.

"First, you look beautiful," he said, running his fingers through my growing hair. "Second, I'm so sorry for not answering your calls, I just—"

"Don't apologize. This whole mess is my fault. I should've told you about Dean—I should have trusted you."

"We both should have handled ourselves better" he held my face in his hands. "Being away from you made me realize that drama or no drama, nothing was right without you. Nothing *is* right without you. Can we just start over?"

"I don't know. I'm just—"

"Give me one second."

He turned his back then quickly faced me again.

"Hello, beautiful. My name is Vince Parker and you are?"

I gazed at his extended hand. Followed the line of his fingers up to his elbow…to his shoulder…the chocolate skin at his neck…the full lips pulled into a mischievous smile.

Can you really give him up? Do you--

To finish the thought was pointless. I knew the answer without having to think it through. I placed my hand in his. Ran my thumb across his knuckles and smiled.

"I'm Sasha. Nice to meet you."

Thank you!

My heartfelt thanks and appreciation goes out to everyone who made this book possible. I'm so grateful you took the time to read this story, and I'D love to hear your thoughts about Sasha and Vince. Please consider leaving a review or contacting me through the sites below:

www.valeribeatrix.com
www.instagram.com/authorvaleribeatrix

Made in the USA
Columbia, SC
11 May 2019